Trace's TROUBLE

Trace's TROUBLE

BY

LEXI POST

TRACE'S TROUBLE
Last Chance Series, Book 2

By Lexi Post

Cowboy Trace Williams thought he had trouble when his wife served him with divorce papers, forcing him to move to his cousin's horse rescue ranch. But that was nothing compared to handling the female squatter he's supposed to evict from Last Chance Ranch. Though she's a crack shot and has no use for politeness or subtlety, her ability to communicate with animals has him seeking her out on behalf of the ranch…and himself.

Whisper Adams lives off the grid. She cares for her invalid uncle and watches over the wildlife that finds her. The animals are more trustworthy than the people she's encountered. So when a hard-bodied, easy going cowboy arrives at her trailer and causes her heart to race, she's anxious for him to leave, until he asks for her help at the ranch.

Since they end up together more often than she prefers, Whisper doesn't deny her attraction to Trace, who introduces her to new experiences, from riding horses to an erotic night in bed. But mixing with people, any people, opens her to new threats. This relationship might cost Trace his heart, but it could very well cost Whisper her life.

Acknowledgments

For Bob Fabich, Sr., who accepts me as I am, the good parts and the flawed. And for my sister Paige Wood, whose honesty is both rewarding and humbling.

Thank you to Teresa Fordice for giving me the name for Black Jack and sharing her story about the horse she loved.

Also, thank you to my beta reader Eileen McCall for her expert eye and fast turn-around. Your feedback made the epilogue possible.

Huge kudos go to my critique partner, Marie Patrick, who critiqued these pages as quickly as I could write them, making it possible to meet my deadline.

Lastly, thank you to Grace Bradley, a wonderful editor and a great friend.

Author's Note

Trace's Trouble was inspired by Bret Harte's short story, "Miggles," first published sometime between 1868 and 1872. In Harte's story, the stagecoach can't cross the swollen river because the bridge is out. Therefore, the passengers seek shelter at Miggles' house.

Miggles is a former prostitute who sold her saloon and bought a place where she could take care of Jim, one of her dying clients, who sits unresponsive in the living room. The six men from the coach find Miggles incredibly attractive and rush to help her whenever she asks. During dinner, her watch dog makes himself known outside so she offers to introduce him to everyone, but when she opens the door, they discover her watch dog is a half-grown bear. The two ladies in the party decide by then that Miggles is beneath them.

Miggles provides dinner for everyone, but when it's time for bed and she shows the women to her room, they make Miggles feel unwelcome, so she sleeps at the foot of her patient in the living room where the men have bedded down. The following morning, she is gone and the men say goodbye to Jim, but linger in the hopes of seeing Miggles one more time. Finally, they board the stagecoach and leave.

On their way down the road, the coachman pulls up on the horses suddenly because on the crest of a nearby hill, is Miggles, her hair blowing in the wind and smiling as she waves a white handkerchief goodbye. When the stage stops at the next town, the men file into the local saloon, get a drink and the judge among them makes a toast to Miggles.

But what if Miggles was an outsider for a different reason, yet she still cared for an older invalid man and got along well with nature's creatures? Could she find acceptance in today's society if she found the right man? Would he delve beneath appearances or would he make an erroneous judgement about such a unique woman?

Chapter One

"Stop right there unless you'd like your head blown off."

At the husky voice, Trace froze, bringing Lightyear to a halt as his gaze swung to the barrel of a rifle barely visible behind the single boulder amidst the Joshua trees and sagebrush. There wasn't supposed to be anyone out here except a woman with a trailer, and so far he'd seen neither. Drug dealers? Coyotes? His right hand itched to grasp his rifle from its scabbard attached to Lightyear's saddle.

He studied the area past the rock. Were there more? There was no other place to hide so completely. He didn't see anyone else. One delinquent he could handle. "Just out for a ride." He smiled crookedly. "Enjoying the day."

"Then turn around and enjoy the day somewhere else." The voice came again, but the rifle barrel remained steady. Whoever held that gun was in his element.

Shit. First he's tasked with doing Cole's dirty work, and then he has to come across some territorial drifter. He frowned at his remembered conversation with Cole.

"You want me to do what?" He tipped his cowboy hat up to stare at his cousin as if he'd just sprouted six legs and a long, poisonous tail.

Cole had the decency to look uncomfortable and lowered his leg from the rail of the training corral. "I don't have a choice. If she's been up there too long she could claim the land as hers under Arizona squatter laws. This Whisper woman needs to move her trailer off our land. You know the boundaries. She probably won't have to move very far. She's up over the rim of the north canyon."

Trace had little sympathy for the opposite sex at the moment, including his soon-to-be ex-wife, but he couldn't see kicking the woman off their land when she'd just saved Lacey's life. Didn't really speak of gratefulness to him. "Does Lacey agree with you?"

Cole started to turn. "It doesn't matter. It's what needs to be done."

Trace stepped in front of his cousin, not the least bit intimidated by Cole's scowl. "You can at least wait until after New Year's. Shit, with this kind of 'thank you,' you'll be lucky if the woman doesn't seek us out and kill us all in our beds."

"Just do it." His cousin stepped around him and strode toward the house.

There was no way this scenario was going to go well for Cole and possibly for the rest of them. To hear Lacey talk about Whisper, the woman walked on water, able to shoot a flower bud on a saguaro cactus from a half mile away.

Trace pulled off his hat and wiped the sweat from his forehead with his bandana then stuffed it back in his pocket and lowered his Stetson. He liked Lacey. She seemed to be a decent woman, one of the few left. She was going to be fit to be tied.

He grinned. Now that was something he'd like to see. It would serve Cole right for being so ungrateful and sending him to do the dirty work. Trace turned back toward the corral to find Lightyear, the mahogany-colored bay with black points that he liked to ride, standing near him. Ignoring the horse's face, he patted its withers. "I guess you and I are going to cause some trouble, boy."

The horse shook its head to dislodge a fly, but Trace chuckled. "No, not for us, but for your righteous owner." He entered the corral and carefully bridled Lightyear with a unique technique he'd developed. The horse was far too sensitive around his face, thanks to an encounter with a traveling swarm of bees.

Lightyear's face had swelled so much he could barely breathe. His owner had left him for dead, but a caring neighbor had called animal welfare. Cole and his vet had nursed the poor horse back to health over a year ago, but it still couldn't stand having its face touched.

Once Trace had the bridle in place, he added the saddle blanket, saddle and cinched the strap. Patting the horse on his side one more time, he mounted.

"Let's get this over with, buddy." Trace kicked Lightyear into a trot and they headed out to the canyon. His cousin had a big heart for horses, but when it came to people who didn't toe the line, he had no give at all.

Too bad Trace hadn't had the same strict rules for right and wrong as Cole had. Instead, he'd been blinded by a love that wasn't reciprocated and would soon lose everything he'd worked so hard for. He should have known. He would never get involved with a down-on-her-luck woman again.

In the meantime, he had a roof over his head and a job he enjoyed. Most of the time.

Now wasn't one of those times.

"Today would be nice. I got better things to do than shoot and bury trespassers. Turn your fancy ass around and get out of here." Though the voice definitely sounded irritated now, he smiled inside at the man's confidence.

Careful to keep his hands still, Trace cocked his head. "Then we have a problem. You see, this is my cousin's land and I'm not the one trespassing."

After a minute or two of no response, but with the rifle barrel still steady, Trace slowly moved his right hand down by his leg. The problem was, even if he did get to the rifle, he was a sitting duck up on Lightyear.

"Who's this supposed cousin?"

At the question, he stilled. Maybe he wasn't talking to a criminal. This could well be the husband of Lacey's Whisper. Preferring to settle the issue peaceably with no one getting hurt, most especially himself, he leaned forward in the saddle, hiding his right hand completely from view. "Cole Hatcher. His fiancée Lacey was up here recently."

"No, she wasn't."

Ah, the man knew who Lacey was. Trace listened intently as a muted swearing and grumbling came from behind the rock. He couldn't quite make out any particular words except "hell."

Grasping the rifle in his hand, he gave Lightyear a tap with his right foot. The horse started to move forward.

"I said turn around!"

Trace moved his left hand toward Lightyear's face. "Whoa, it's okay, buddy." He scratched beneath the horse's ear and Lightyear reared. Gripping the horse with his knees, he swung the rifle around and shot the rock where the barrel was visible.

"Dammit." The barrel moved then. "Freaking-a, what the hell are you doing? I could have shot you."

He still felt like a sitting duck, but since the man hadn't shot him yet, it meant he wasn't trigger-happy. "Show yourself."

A laugh sounded from behind the boulder. A very husky, feminine laugh and Trace's pulse accelerated.

"Now why would I do that?"

The voice was no different, but as Trace imagined a woman instead of a man, it no longer felt threatening. Instead, it had his imagination running wild without any clothes. Intrigued, his curiosity got the best of him. "Are you Whisper?"

The silence was deafening and he brought the rifle up again. He may have imagined that feminine tone. He hadn't been with a woman since he was served the papers for the divorce. He should probably find himself a one-night stand soon or he'd be thinking the fence post was a woman.

"Who wants to know?"

"I'm Trace, Cole's cousin. He sent me up here to talk to you."

Again silence. There was no way the rifle-bearer was a woman. Women weren't that patient, or that quiet, at least not in his experience.

A figure unfolded itself from behind the rock and Trace's breath got stuck in his lungs. Startling silver eyes peered at him from beneath a worn, brown-leather cowboy hat. Beneath those eyes was a straight, elegant nose, high cheekbones and full lips that remained closed. A stubborn jaw anchored the lower face while small wisps of black hair framed the sides, the rest tied back somehow.

"So talk."

Trace blinked, letting the rifle go slack. As he took in the rest of the image, his interest cooled. The woman wore a loose red-and-black flannel shirt, a brown leather vest, a handgun stuffed into the waist of her baggy jeans and square-toed cowboy boots that had seen better days. Alarm bells went off in his head. A down-on-her-luck woman. Shit. "Are you Whisper?"

Her nod was barely discernable.

"Hello, miss. I understand you have a trailer up here."

Again, a slight nod.

He wasn't used to silent women. His wife talked nonstop, mostly about what she needed. Lacey, who he actually thought was a decent woman, also needed to fill in the silence as well, but at least with important stuff.

His task was important, at least to Cole. "Can I see it?"

"Why?"

So I can tell you it's on Hatcher-Williams land and you need to move it. He glanced down at the rifle held loosely in her hand. Lacey's comments on what a great shot Whisper was had him rethinking his plan. Maybe the straightforward approach wasn't the best. "Lacey said you lived up here with someone."

"Yeah, my uncle." She still didn't move, but her gaze flicked between him and Lightyear.

Interesting. "Can I talk to him?" Maybe a man-to-man conversation would be easier.

Her lips quirked up on one side just slightly, just enough to rivet his gaze. "Sure. This way."

Trace took a moment to get Lightyear moving, his mind still stuck on the image of her full, feminine lips, but once he set the horse to a walk in between the Joshua trees, it became apparent that riding wasn't the easiest way to move forward.

Quickly, he jumped down and carefully pulled the reins over Lightyear's head so they wouldn't brush along the horse's face. He grasped them low and guided the horse between trees, keeping the blue jeans and brown vest in sight.

Whisper's long, straight black ponytail swished back-and-forth with her stride, catching his attention and holding it to the point he almost walked into a prickly pear cactus. Shit, as if the Joshua trees didn't make this area of the high desert a challenge enough to navigate. No wonder he and his cousin had rarely ventured up here as kids. How the hell did they get a trailer in here?

Finally, they emerged into what looked like a natural clearing of hard-packed earth and there sat a large trailer covered in the dust of the environment. In front of it sat a single Adirondack chair and a chiminea. With a quick scan, he could see a shed to the left and slightly behind it, a cord running to the trailer. A generator? To the right of the home sat an ATV under the shade of a wooden carport-type structure.

"He's in there." Whisper grabbed his attention once again and he raised an eyebrow. "You're not coming in?"

"It's too close in there with more than two people." She waved her hand toward the trailer even as she sat in the chair, the rifle on her lap. "Go ahead. You can introduce yourself."

Trace released Lightyear's reins. "Stay there, buddy. I'll be right back." Anxious to talk to a man instead of Lacey's odd friend, Trace strode quickly to the trailer and knocked.

"Oh, go ahead in. Uncle Joey won't bite."

Then why did he suddenly have the feeling she wasn't giving him the whole story. Opening the trailer door, he stepped inside and took off his hat. His first impression was Christmas from a cheap department store had dumped into the large space. The second was that it was a lot roomier than he expected and a lot nicer. His third impression was that the man with his back to him might be hard of hearing because he didn't turn at his entrance.

Trace cleared his throat loudly, so as not to startle the white-haired gentleman as he walked to the chair directly across from him. He turned, extending his hand. "Howdy, sir, I'm Trace Williams."

When the man looked at him but didn't move, Trace noticed more. The pale-blue eyes staring back at him were sharp, but the rest of the face sagged on the left side. The hair was neatly trimmed, but thin, and the entire visage was marked by sunspots and wrinkles, common among the elderly in Arizona. Both arms lay in the man's lap, relaxed.

Something was seriously wrong here. "I understand you're Whisper's uncle, Joey." He raised his voice.

The man squinted a tiny bit before he gave a small jerk of his head, which was obviously a nod.

So the man was not deaf at all. "May I?" He pointed to the chair.

Uncle Joey gave another jerk of his head.

Clearly the man had suffered a stroke, but was still all there. A strong sympathy for Joey's plight had Trace searching for alternatives to his mandated task. He couldn't imagine what it must be like to be in Joey's shoes. He looked the man in the eyes. "I wanted to meet you. Did you know your niece saved my cousin's fiancée?"

Joey gave a jerk of his head again, but his gaze made it clear he was pretty proud of Whisper.

An unforeseen curiosity got the better of Trace. "Did you raise Whisper?"

The man's mouth opened on one side then he rolled his eyes.

Trace grinned. "So she was a handful, huh?"

Joey jerked his head again.

"I have to tell you, that doesn't surprise me. What happened to her parents?"

Joey looked down then returned his gaze to Trace's.

"Okay, I'm guessing they died. Was it an accident?"

Again the older man's head jerked.

He could tell Joey was enjoying their "conversation" so he kept at it. "And she was pretty young?"

The man jerked again and gave a short grunt.

"Hmm, so young. So not a teenager yet?"

Joey's eyes lit with pleasure and he jerked his head again, his mouth partially open.

Trace was thoroughly enjoying himself as he learned Uncle Joey's mannerisms. It was similar to understanding a horse. Cole could go to hell. There was no way *he* was kicking these people off the land.

"So how long have you two been up here? A long time?"

Joey didn't move at all.

Trace relaxed. Maybe there was no need for them to move.

"So somewhat recently. Hmm." The shed and ATV cover said it had at least been months. "Would you say less than a year?"

Joey didn't move.

Damn. "Would you say under two years?"

Joey jerked his head.

He was no expert on squatter rights, but for some reason the two-year mark made him uncomfortable, like he'd heard that timeframe before.

Joey's eyes flitted to his right and Trace turned his head to look out the large window facing the "front yard" of the home. His jaw dropped.

Whisper was with Lightyear, stroking his nose and cheek, talking to him. He looked back at Joey. "That horse can't stand anything touching his face. How is she doing that?"

Joey's eyes lit with pride once more, but the only sound he made was a short grunt. Trace got the feeling Whisper's uncle wasn't surprised in the least.

Maybe he should be bringing Lightyear up here for his training. He turned back to watch Whisper. Her connection with his horse reminded him of Lacey's connection to Angel, but she'd formed that over months.

"She's good with horses, isn't she?"

He glanced back to Joey to see him jerk his head. Then he moved his eyes up and down.

What could that mean? "She's had many horses?"

Joey didn't move.

"She likes to ride horses?"

Joey rolled his eyes.

Trace laughed. "I'm not very good at this, am I?"

The older man jerked his head and his mouth opened, which Trace was pretty sure was the closest he could get to a smile.

The door opened. "What's going on in here?"

The cowboy, Trace, looked at her as if he'd been caught doing something he shouldn't. Then he moved his gaze to Joey and chuckled.

Whisper's stomach tightened. *Uncle Joey was hers.* Even at the thought, she recognized it for being silly, childish and selfish, but he was and always had been. She didn't want some drop-dead gorgeous, hunky cowboy with short sun-streaked brown hair and warm reddish-brown eyes muscling in on her territory. "You can leave now." Damn. Even to her that sounded rude. "Uncle Joey isn't used to so much stimulation."

Trace returned his copper gaze to her and her heart hiccupped. It'd been doing that ever since she stood up from behind the boulder and met him face-to-face. She didn't like the feeling at all.

Joey grunted.

She looked at Joey. "Don't you go giving me any lip now, old man."

Trace stood and bowed toward her uncle. "It's been a pleasure chatting with you. Hope we can do it again sometime."

Her traitorous uncle jerked his head before the tall cowboy walked toward her. Though the trailer was spacious for her and Joey, Trace took up too much space. He was taller and broader than she was and solid muscle, at least that's how it appeared from the outline of his clothes.

She backed up into the kitchen to let him proceed outside. But instead, he donned his cowboy hat and waved her toward the door.

She gave an exaggerated sigh and opened the latch, stepping down onto the hard-packed earth.

When the cowboy closed the door, she turned on him, a

smirk curling her lip. "So, did you find out everything you came up here for?"

The man studied her, his eyes hidden by the shadow of his hat. "Yes I did, thank you."

Huh? "Good. Now you can go."

He cocked his head. "I would think with no one around for miles you wouldn't mind a little company for a change."

"Nope." At least not his. He had her stomach in knots and she didn't like it. "Not real partial to people. Animals are much better company."

Trace laughed at her statement, sending a pleasant sensation over her body, like the sprinkle of a light rain.

"I have to admit to having that thought a time or two, especially in the ranch house. But the barn can be peaceful, even soothing. I like listening to the sound of a horse munching on dinner while another chuffs and moves around in the shavings." He looked off in the distance as if seeing every detail. "As dusk comes on, you can hear the crickets, and the desert mice scampering back into their nests." His gaze locked with hers. "Nature is more straightforward than man."

Feeling a sense of kinship with him at his description, it took her a moment to catch the undertone of bitterness in his final statement. Her mind eased as she sensed he might understand. "Yeah, I get that. A horse lets you know exactly how she feels. You also know how a coyote or mountain lion feels the second you find yourself in their company."

He grinned. "You in the company of those animals often up here?"

She shrugged. "Faust comes by when he's hungry and—" At his intent stare, she halted. "Anyway, you were leaving, right?"

"Yes, but not right away. I find the company up here far too fascinating."

She glanced back at the trailer for a moment before nodding. "Yeah, Uncle Joey's a hoot."

"I enjoyed chatting with him. He said you two have been up here almost two years."

He got that from Joey? Her defenses went up as fast as a rat trap. "Maybe."

He pointed at the shed. "I figured it was a decent amount of time from the looks of that shed. That would have taken time to build and it's a bit weathered."

This cowboy was a little too observant for her comfort.

"How'd you get all the wood here? Do you have something you hitch to your ATV?"

She shrugged, not in a hurry to reveal any more than he'd already guessed. She didn't need him to be poking around in her background. Last time someone did that, her two deadbeat cousins had come after her within hours. According to her parents' will, if she was incapacitated, Timmy and Keith would inherit all the money except what was needed to care for her, so she and Joey had had to move again. She didn't want that happening again. She really liked this area of the state.

When she didn't answer, Trace strode toward the front of the trailer where she had the ATV parked.

"What are you looking for?"

This time *he* didn't answer. Instead, he ducked under the ATV shelter and examined the trailer hitch.

It was definitely time for him to leave. "Hey, I got some chores to do. If you're done visiting, I'm fine with you leaving." She got his attention with that.

His head snapped up. "You really don't like people, do you?"

It was more that she didn't like what people wanted from her or how he—they—made her feel. "No, I don't."

He backed up. "I apologize. I was just curious. Your lifestyle is, well, admirable. I think I'm a bit jealous. I forgot about how rewarding a simple life could be. Having your own place and the open desert all to yourself is a bit of heaven."

Heaven? Yeah, it was kind of like that. She'd never met anyone else who understood.

Trace took a bandana from his back pocket and lifted his hat to wipe his forehead, then returned the cloth to where it belonged. "How did you get the trailer out here?"

She shrugged. He may appreciate her lifestyle, but he asked too many questions. She left her truck in town with the vet. Dr. Jenna used it when she needed to transport larger animals in return for keeping it safe and out of the dry desert environment.

The arrangement had the additional benefit of keeping Whisper's cousins off her trail. They'd come through town shortly after she arrived, asking about her. Jenna told them she'd seen Whisper head west, mainly because Whisper was in the office with a sick gray fox at the time and Jenna didn't like the look of them.

All Whisper needed was the ATV most of the time anyway.

Trace studied her, his eyes visible now that he stood on the shady side of her home. His face was too damn handsome. Far more rugged and mature than the boyfriend she'd had when she was a teenager.

"Whisper, you can trust me. You don't need to hide from me."

She'd learned from her two cousins not to trust men, except for Joey, who had looked out for her, kept her safe. Uncle Joey was different. "I'm not hiding. I'm just living. Me and Joey are good. Why did you come here?"

Trace looked away. "My cousin asked me to. He was

curious about the woman who saved Lacey. You made quite an impression on her. She admires you a lot."

Why did he keep saying nice things? "Lacey's a good person."

He grinned. "That she is." His tone turned bitter and he shifted his weight, scraping the heel of his boot in the dirt. "One of the few women I can say that about."

She wanted to know what a woman had done to him because it was obvious he'd been on the short end of that stick. Her curiosity caught her off guard. Why should she want to know anything? He was just a nosey cowboy.

"Don't you want to know what happened after Cole brought her home?" Trace was back to studying her.

"What do you mean?" Obviously, they got home safe.

"I mean Ray Norton, the bastard who beat Angel within inches of her life. The man you shot up."

Anger surged through her as she grasped who he meant. "I hope he died."

"I wish." Trace shook his head. "He's still alive, but you'll be happy to know he'll never walk again without a limp."

"Not good enough." She clamped her mouth shut before she said any more.

Trace's lips lifted up into a sympathetic smile. "My feelings exactly."

She started to smile, but caught herself. He agreed with too much. She glanced down at his dirty boots. They were in excellent shape beneath the dust. His boots were too nice. Nope, she didn't trust him as far as she could throw him.

She turned away, not willing to let him see her face. Maybe if she—

A screech, followed by a scuffle sounded near the shed. "God damn eagle!" She raced toward the creosote bush and quickly spotted the dust and flapping feathers. "Go pick on someone your own size!" Her heart beat hard as she swatted at the golden eagle trying to grab the baby jackrabbit.

Trace's cowboy hat hit the eagle in its chest and it finally backed off. She crouched to pick up the baby, careful to avoid touching the long cut along the side of her large ear.

"Shoo." Trace walked by her, but she ignored him as she checked Viola for other injuries. It looked like the scratch was the only wound. She could save her. She looked over the ground for Sebastian. He was gone, probably scared off. Shit.

"That eagle is going to be pretty hungry."

She stared at the black boots in front of her but refused to be drawn in. Instead, she rose with the baby rabbit and headed for the trailer.

"Whisper, you know it's nature's way." His voice saying her name buried itself in her brain. Something she could think about later.

"Go away. I'm busy." She needed to get Viola's scratch cleaned, keep her warm and watch for shock. Jackrabbits depended on their ears and this one was barely a few days old. She also needed to find Sebastian. He would be lonely without Viola. She opened the door to the trailer, trying to remember where she'd stored the empty box from the coffeemaker she bought last month.

"You're welcome." Trace's hard voice made her hesitate.

She looked back over her shoulder. Trace had re-donned his hat, his body stiff. The life of an animal was far more important than a man's feelings. But despite her best intentions, she nodded. "Thank you." She let the door slam behind her.

Chapter Two

Trace stared at the closed door. That had to be oddest conversation he'd ever had with a woman, with anyone. He'd prided himself on his charm when he was younger. So much so he'd been blindsided by Yvonne. So engrossed in charming her from her shyness, he'd failed to see it was all an act. He'd thought of himself as her knight in shining armor.

Trace grunted as he carefully looped the reins over the pommel and mounted Lightyear. His armor was pretty tarnished now, not to mention bent in too many places to be repaired. It was time to dump it.

Clicking Lightyear into a walk, he headed back to the rim. Despite his mixed feelings about asking Whisper to leave Cole's land, once he'd met Joey, he refused to say anything. He may be a fallen knight, but he wasn't heartless. Neither was his cousin. He was confident he could get Cole to let them stay.

As he crested the rim, he allowed Lightyear to pick his own way down the canyon wall. He had complete faith in the animal even though he had to lean far back in the saddle in a couple places that were seriously steep. He still couldn't believe Whisper had touched Lightyear's face. When he got back to the barn, he'd try it to see if she'd worked some kind of magic.

As they reached the bottom of the wall, he gave Lightyear his head. The quarter horse was named after the speed of light for a reason. According to Cole, he was bred from two racers. Trace just couldn't imagine anyone giving up on such an amazing animal. A tinge of guilt kicked his conscience. He'd had a couple dozen horses, but even now he couldn't remember their names. The cowboys who worked for him had taken care of them. He'd lost touch with his roots, trying to achieve what he thought was success. He'd become a rancher and left his real cowboy boots to gather dust.

As he passed Cole and Lacey's new construction, he couldn't help but think of the sprawling ranch house he used to own. When he'd built the giant stone fireplace, he had envisioned nights cuddled up with his wife before a roaring fire, but that never happened. There was never time.

His mother said his rising star had risen too fast. Maybe she was right, but he sure as hell would have liked to at least be able to afford an apartment now. Maybe once the final papers were signed, he'd have something left after the lawyer took his percentage.

As he rode up to the barn, his brother, Logan, walked Tiny Dancer toward the corral. The young paint stepped gingerly and seemed to breathe a sigh of relief once she was left to her own devices.

Logan had let his hair grow longer, but he still looked hard and grumpy. He held Tiny Dancer's halter in his hand as he stepped up to meet him. "Were you successful in ousting the squatters?"

Trace halted Lightyear. "I'm not sure they're squatters. I think Cole needs to hear the whole story."

Logan shook his head. "Don't know why he sent you to play the bully. If he'd sent me, they'd be long gone by now."

"No, they wouldn't." Trace's gut tensed with growing anger. "You would have been back here in fifteen minutes with a bullet wound. That woman greeted me with the barrel of a rifle."

Logan laughed. "I guess you still have the Williams' charm then because I don't see any bullet holes in you."

His anger eased. "Nope, and I found out a lot about our outlying tenants that Cole will find very interesting."

"Whoa, if your goal is to let them stay, good luck with that." Logan patted Lightyear on his side and turned toward the house.

Trace urged the horse toward the barn. He had no doubt he could help Whisper and Joey. All he needed to do was talk to Lacey. Between the two of them, Cole didn't stand a chance.

After jumping down from Lightyear, he led him into his stall and carefully removed the bridle before unsaddling him. He pulled a pitchfork from the wall and gave the horse a healthy lunch. "There you go, buddy."

He hung up the pitchfork and headed toward the barn door then halted. He was far too curious about Whisper to let go of the fact that she patted Lightyear on the face. Letting himself into the stall, he barely laid his hand on Lightyear's nose as he ate. The horse threw its head up and neighed.

"Sorry, buddy, I just had to check." With a secret smile on his face, Trace let himself out of the barn and headed for the main house. Now he had more ammunition against Cole.

As he stepped inside, his grandmother's voice from the kitchen greeted him.

"I think that's a wonderful idea, but how many were you hoping to invite? I'm not sure we can fit many more."

He walked in, nodded to his grandfather and gave his grandmother a kiss on the cheek. "Many more what?"

Lacey and Cole stood near the fridge. Cole wasn't in his

fire department shirt for a change, but he still looked huge next to his delicate wife. It was all that gym equipment at the station. Lacey wore a button-down blouse and long skirt, probably because she had to work later today. Her blonde hair was neatly braided on one side and the two lovebirds held hands as usual. He couldn't remember his wife holding his hand. Did they even do that while dating?

Lacey beamed at him. "We're throwing a New Year's Eve party." She switched her gaze to his grandmother. "I was actually thinking we could have it in our partially finished house. Cole said we could get one of those heaters they use with tents when it's too cold outside, and we can rent tables and chairs. I was thinking of having it catered."

His grandmother set down her ice tea in surprise. "That's actually not a bad idea. You have no walls dividing the rooms yet so we could even dance."

Lacey looked at Cole. "Do you think we could have a DJ? The plywood floors would be perfect for dancing."

Cole kissed Lacey on the forehead. "Of course, what would a New Year's Eve party be without dancing?" His brow furrowed. "I'm just not sure who we can get for the catering or the DJ on such late notice. It's only three days away."

Trace listened for a few minutes as the four discussed possibilities then quietly backed out of the room. He'd probably be asked to help with setup and maybe a few errands, but as far as planning, they didn't need him. Just like his wife's parties. She hadn't wanted his input in the planning, though he did make sure he was there. He'd been so concerned about someone else catching her eye that he failed to realize her eye was on his bank account, not his guests.

As he stepped out onto the porch, a truck pulled into the ranch with a trailer hitched to it. He'd learned from Cole shortly after moving to Last Chance that a truck and trailer was cause for excitement. Either a horse was being brought for rehabilitation or it was a potential buyer who didn't know Cole insisted on checking out the future homes of his horses.

Trace jumped down the stairs and met the driver. An older cowboy stepped out. "Howdy, I'm Don. Animal Welfare sent me to drop off these two horses."

Trace looked back toward the trailer. "Two?"

Don started to walk to the back. "Yeah. There's actually three in total, but one wasn't ready to travel yet. The vet's watching her overnight."

Trace helped Don lower the ramp. "Why have they come here?"

Don halted. "Starvation. The family of five came upon hard times and instead of selling their 'beloved' horses, they just stopped feeding them. They said they thought the grass would be enough." He spat on the ground. "You should have seen the place. There wasn't a blade of green left."

Trace braced himself as Don backed a gray Palomino out of the trailer. The horse's ribs were so well defined that Trace had to swallow to keep his anger from boiling out. It was important to stay calm around the new horses. Glancing over at the closest corral, he was glad to find it empty. "Let's bring him over here."

Don looked at him. "You don't want him in the barn?"

"Not yet." Trace walked with the man. "We need to evaluate him first."

Don shrugged and handed the reins to Trace. "Then you take him and I'll get the other."

Trace entered the corral with the gray. The horse's eyes looked dull, as if he'd given up hope of ever having a decent meal, and he had a minimal hair coat despite the cooler temperatures this time of year.

Trace looked up from his examination to see Don leading what would have been a handsome Missouri Fox Trotter if the horse had any energy at all. Instead, the horse's head hung low, its blond mane filled with brambles and its café au lait coat dirty.

Don handed the reins over to Trace, and he brought the animal in. Taking off the halter, he climbed over the fence to face Don. "What are their names?"

"I have the paperwork in the truck."

As they headed for the man's vehicle, Logan strode out of the house. "More horses?"

Trace motioned toward the corral. "Take a look."

Don pulled the paperwork from the front seat and sifted through it. "Storm is the gray Palomino. The Missouri Fox Trotter is Rogue and the mare that is still to come is…" The man shuffled through the papers. "Ah, here it is. Mystique." The cowboy frowned. "Strange name for a horse if you ask me."

Trace grinned. Not so strange if the family of five had three children into comics.

"Are you Cole Hatcher?"

Trace glanced toward the house to see Cole and Lacey coming outside. "No, but this man is. I'll let him take it from here."

Trace passed by Cole on his way to catch Lacey. "You still have another coming."

Cole nodded as he passed.

Lacey stood at the edge of the porch, watching his cousin. Trace bounded up the steps and stood next to her. "How's it going, Blondie?"

She didn't look at him. "It was going great until these poor horses arrived. How could anyone do this to such magnificent creatures?"

Trace agreed with her, but then again, he'd never had to

choose between giving up his horses and feeding his kids. His horses had been taken from him, he had no children, and he was homeless, so it was a moot point. "Not everyone was meant to own them."

Lacey looked at him. "That's an understatement."

"Now, your friend Whisper would never let a horse starve. I bet she'd give a horse her last meal if that's what it took."

"Whisper?" Lacey was staring at him now. "What about her?"

He shrugged. "Nothing. By the way, she says hello."

"Trace Williams, what did you do to her?" Lacey leaned toward him, her brows furrowed.

He kept his grin to himself and held up his hands, backing up a step in mock fright. "Whoa, settle down there, I was just passing on a message."

Lacey advanced. "But you saw her. Did you find where she lives?"

He nodded. "Yes, ma'am. I found her just like Cole wanted me to."

Lacey halted her progress. "Cole?"

At the look on Lacey's face, Trace felt a twinge of guilt, but at his remembered conversation with Joey, and Whisper's affection for Lightyear, he pushed his advantage. "Yes. He sent me up over the rim to find her. She takes care of her uncle who appears to have had a stroke. He is completely dependent on her."

Lacey's gaze softened. "I knew it."

"Knew what?"

She smiled. "I knew she had a good heart, but she's been hurt. Did she say anything about her family?"

Family? Trace hadn't even considered there might be someone else living there. Whisper could have a husband for all he knew and that was why there was no truck there because the man of the house was at work. Actually, that made a lot of sense since the trailer couldn't have been pulled in there with the ATV.

He didn't like that her husband would leave her out in the desert alone with her uncle like that.

"Trace? Did you hear me?"

He refocused his attention on Lacey. "I don't know if she has a husband. She didn't mention one."

Lacey gave him an odd look. "You have to show me where she lives. I need to talk to her."

He'd like nothing more but didn't want to press his luck with his cousin. After all, it was only because of Cole and his grandparents that he had a roof over his head. "I'd be happy to, but you should probably talk to your fiancé first. He's not too happy about her living up there."

"Why not?"

"You'll have to ask him."

"What aren't you telling me, Trace?" Lacey took a step closer.

"No way, Blondie. That's a conversation between you and Cole. I was just delivering a message." He backed up another step and opened the door to the house. If he didn't miss his guess, he and Lacey would be riding up to Whisper's trailer by tomorrow afternoon.

He wasn't sure why he looked forward to that visit, but he did.

~~*~~

Whisper closed the book of Shakespeare comedies. She'd read from *Twelfth Night* in honor of her two guest rabbits. She'd named them after the comedy about twins, since they were almost impossible to tell apart, until Viola got scratched.

After setting the book on the side table next to Joey's bed, she pressed the button that elevated his head six inches higher. He slept much better that way.

Satisfied with the height, she stepped over to the small box on the kitchen floor and checked on Viola and Sebastian. When she'd finished getting Viola settled earlier, she'd gone back to the scene of the trauma and found Sebastian cowering under the shed. Now the two babies slept on top of each other, finding comfort in their companionship.

Pulling her coat off the hook by the door, she put it on before sticking Sal into the waistband of her jeans. The Glock came in handy if a rattler got too close. Stepping to the fridge, she pulled out a beer, popped the cap and took a swig. Hmm, the perfect ending to an interesting day. Walking to the door, she quietly let herself out.

Once outside, she settled herself in her chair and buttoned her coat. The temperatures were dropping lower at night, leaving a frost on the desert floor in the morning. She looked at the chiminea, the ash from her last fire still inside. She didn't feel like making a fire. It wasn't cold enough to expend that kind of effort.

Taking another swallow of beer, she leaned her head back and stared at the sky. She watched and waited for the first shooting star of the night. Minutes went by before one finally streaked across the heavens and burned up on the horizon.

Some people believed the stars were good omens and others thought them bad. With the number of shooting stars out in the desert in Arizona, she thought it safe to bet they meant nothing in the grand scheme of tiny men's lives.

Not that she'd had many men in her life. Her dad, her Uncle Joey, and her teenage boyfriend were pretty much it. She saw nothing wrong with that until this morning when Trace decided to mosey on into her life.

She allowed herself a slow smile. The man was sexy, not that she'd ever let him know that. He made her insides all squishy and caused her to have a hard time focusing.

Whisper let her eyes close as she pictured Trace when he grinned, his white teeth gleaming against his tan face. The dark stubble around his lips and his chin just made him appear more rugged. Despite his new clothes and boots, she sensed a strength of purpose in him. That and just brute animal strength.

She opened her eyes. Is that why she felt comfortable around him? Because she could relate to the animal side of him? Hmm. She closed her eyes again. That was an interesting observation. The fact was, his animal side was pure male. Large forearms visible below his rolled-up sleeves attested to that. She'd love to see him without a shirt on.

He'd have a stomach like an old washboard and chest muscles that rivaled a martial arts expert. His jeans had been tight and she hadn't missed what a great ass he had as he leaned over to check out the trailer hitch.

She wouldn't mind hitching her wagon to him any day…in her dreams. They were almost the same height with him maybe a couple inches taller. She liked that. At six feet, she was taller than some men.

They could throw a blanket down under the stars and take off their clothes. She flushed. Would he find her enticing? She would love to just look at him in the moonlight. His body would be hard, strong, making her tingle with the thought of pressing herself against him, flesh to flesh. He would be gentle at first, the part she liked. He could cup her breasts in his large hands and his thumbs could stroke across her nipples. Sharp pings of pleasure would flow from there straight to her vagina.

She loved the tightness she would feel as her nipples were fondled. He could lower his mouth, still holding her breasts aloft, and lick each nipple before biting lightly, making her knees weak. Then he could suck, his mouth encapsulating her whole nipple, tugging at her. She would grasp his shoulders to keep herself upright.

While his mouth continued its homage to her breast, his hand would sneak down to find the black curls that hid her sex. His finger would spread her nether lips and seek out her opening. Her knees would give way and he'd gently lower her to the blanket, his strong arms cradling her descent.

Once she was laid out before him, he would first spread her hair about her and admire its texture. Her last boyfriend found her long hair mesmerizing. But then Trace would spread her legs as well, wanting to prepare her as much as possible for the inevitable.

Kneeling between her thighs, he would spread her folds and his finger would seek her entrance, slowly gliding inside and then out, mimicking what he would do. But unlike her one other lover, he wouldn't stop there. Having seen how much she enjoyed his attentions to her breasts, he would lean over her and nip at each one.

She'd very much like it if he stayed kneeling and played her nipples between his thumbs and forefingers to distract her with pleasure even as his penis nudged her opening.

The pleasure of her nipples would build the tightness in her womb, making her limbs feel like licorice in the hot sun. She'd float in the pleasure of weightlessness.

Then Trace would plunge himself into her and reality would return. She'd be patient while he rutted and as with an animal, she'd praise him for his performance. Because he was a cowboy, after he pulled out, he might hold her close as if it all meant something special.

Something cold and wet touched her hand and she jerked her eyes open. "Faust."

The coyote sat back on his haunches and stared at her.

"Holy moly, you scared the shit out of me. You shouldn't sneak up on a person when they're daydreaming." She looked the coyote over. He never came so close. He must be seriously hungry.

"Okay, okay, let me see what I have saved up." She stood and the animal backed off. Taking a sip of her beer, she set it on the wide arm of the chair then strolled to the outside compartment that housed a mini-fridge. She took out a plate of scraps she'd saved. "I'll warn you now, there's not much. You've only been gone three days this time."

She walked past her chair and set the plate down, not in the mood to make him beg. That he'd actually touched her bothered her. His cold nose reminded her of the cold feeling she experienced after sex. Walking back to her chair, she sat and watched Faust eat.

Despite the lackluster ending to sex, she could still dream and enjoy the best part. It had been so long, over twelve years. It might be worth the risk to try it again. But first she needed to find out why Trace had been up to visit her in the first place. Her gut told her he hadn't lied, but he also hadn't told the entire truth.

Faust held the plate with his paw as he licked every grease particle from it. She grinned. It was so easy to please animals, give them food, water, shelter if they needed it and a little affection in some cases and they were as happy as a black bear with a salmon.

But people complicated things. They needed money, lots of it and would do anything to get their hands on it, including taking it from a child and lying to their own kin. Most of her greedy relatives finally got on with their lives by time she was ten, but two on her mother's side, Keith and Timmy, did nothing but try to get at her money, legally or illegally.

She thanked her parents every day for leaving her in Uncle Joey's custody. Joey hadn't known anything about raising a child, but as an accountant, he'd known how to protect her inheritance.

Now it was her turn to protect him. She really didn't want to move and Joey liked it here better than any other spot they'd been. She loved it here, too, but if her good deed of helping Lacey on Christmas day brought Trace snooping around one more time, she would probably have to get out the map…again.

A sigh from the coyote caught her attention as he lay down facing her, just a couple yards away. "What would you do if I left?"

Faust's ears turned toward her, but otherwise he didn't move.

"And there's Viola and Sebastian to think about now, plus who knows when Motley is going to return, the ungrateful burro. Nope, I can't leave this spot quite yet. Too many depend on me right now. I'll just have to lay low and avoid Trace as much as possible."

Yup, that's what she'd do. If he showed up again, she'd hide. There was only so much he could get out of Joey and she was pretty sure he had little patience. Men generally didn't have any, so he would eventually go home.

Having settled another weighty life question to her satisfaction, Whisper finished off her beer. "I'm heading to bed, Faust. Keep an eye on the place, will ya?"

The coyote opened one eye as she stood then closed it again.

She smiled. Was there such a thing as a watchcoyote as opposed to a watchdog?

~~*~~

Trace leaned back against Lightyear's stall as the short veterinarian tried to coax Mystique to eat. The chocolate-brown quarter horse hadn't eaten anything by mouth in the last forty-eight hours and they were all concerned. The vet who had kept her overnight had fed her intravenously and while that was still an option, it wasn't the long-term solution they needed.

Cole's vet, Dr. Jenna, was stumped. "There's no medical reason I can find for her not eating."

Logan scowled. "Fine. Then feed her like the last vet did until we can find the solution."

Jenna threw her hands up. "And what's wrong with figuring that out now?"

"Because she's starving *now*."

Lacey placed her hand on Logan's forearm. "Maybe you could go outside and call Cole to give him an update?"

Trace could see what Lacey was doing, diffusing the conflict, and he held his breath until Logan finally nodded. "Fine." He stalked out of the barn, disappearing from view.

Jenna sighed. "Thank you. It's hard to think when every word you say is being challenged."

Lacey smiled. "I figured as much. So what options do we have?"

"That's just it. I've tried everything I know. Maybe we need a horse whisperer." She rolled her eyes and Lacey smirked.

Trace froze as the image of Whisper petting Lightyear streaked across his mind. "It can't hurt to try, right?"

The women turned as one to stare at him. Lacey shrugged. "No, but I'm not sure there is such a person in all of Arizona."

Jenna shook her head. "There are a few who claim to be, but who knows."

Trace pushed off the wall and stood straight, his gut telling him he was right. "I know someone who can help. Whisper."

"Whisper? Why do you say that? I know she's good with a

gun…" She looked at Jenna. "Don't ask. Why do you think she could help with Mystique?"

He grinned as his confidence in the woman's ability rose. "Because I saw her pet Lightyear on his face and he didn't move a muscle."

"What? No way." Lacey's eyes widened.

He nodded. "Yup. And I watched her with my own eyes as she fought off a golden eagle to save two baby jackrabbits. She even told me she's better with animals than with people."

Lacey smiled. "Do you think she'd come? You didn't tell her about Cole's stubborn need to have her move off the land, did you?"

Trace shook his head. "I was hoping you could bring him around."

"And I will. Just give me time."

"We don't have much time with Mystique." Jenna laid her hand on the matted coat of the mare. "I'll have to feed her intravenously like Logan suggested just to keep her alive if she doesn't start eating in the next couple hours. I know Whisper. She brought a couple wild animals into my clinic, but I have no way of getting in contact with her."

Trace stared at the vet. "You know Whisper?"

The woman looked away. "Not well."

She clearly hid something about Whisper and he wanted to know what it was, but the mare's welfare had to take priority. "I can go get her, but if she comes here, I'm sure she's going to want someone to stay with her Uncle Joey."

Lacey clasped her hands again, a nervous habit she had when she was concerned. "That's right, she said she had an uncle. Grandpa's off golfing and he took Billy for his caddy again. What about your grandmother? If Annette goes, do you think Whisper will come?"

He grinned. "If she knows it's to help an animal, I'm ninety percent sure she will."

Logan strode in. "Cole said to do whatever it takes to keep the mare alive."

Trace clapped his brother on the back, his good mood incongruent with the serious circumstances, but he had to admit he was pleased he would be seeing Whisper and Joey again. "So what do you think of watching your baby daughter for a few hours? I want to take grandma to visit someone."

Logan looked wary. "And this helps the horse how?"

"Come back to the house with me and I'll explain."

~~*~~

Though Logan had been doubtful, Trace had complete confidence that Whisper could help. His grandmother rode with him. She had her white-and-gray hair pulled back into a tight bun and she wore a blue sweater and jeans with brown cowboy boots. Though one of those slender older people, she had a spirit that was made of steel and she ruled the roost at Last Chance. It might be why grandpa was forever off golfing, fishing or hunting. Despite grandma's years, she was still an excellent horsewoman and Sadie, her horse, was strong and steady.

He pulled up a hundred yards from the canyon wall and waited for his grandmother to halt next to him.

"The wall is not too difficult for the horses once you get past the shale."

She waved off his words. "I've been up here many times, Trace. Just lead the way."

Of course, he should have known. Kicking Lightyear into a gallop, he headed for the canyon wall. Halfway up, he looked back to see his grandmother had made it past the shale and was close on his heels. It puzzled him his own mother had given up riding so early. Then again, it may have been her financial circumstances. Without dad to run the ranch, and himself too busy with his own spread, her move into town had become a necessity. He'd thought Logan had it all under control. Another misjudgment on his part.

Once he reached the top, he waited for his grandmother then led the way through the Joshua trees. Now that he knew the way, it was just as easy to stay on his horse. He had to grin when he recognized the boulder that Whisper had hidden behind. There was no rifle barrel there now, nor any command to halt.

When they broke into the dry clearing, his grandmother sighed. "I remember this spot. Your grandfather and I camped out here a couple times. How nice that someone else has found it."

"Whisper lives here with her Uncle Joey. I don't know if there is anyone else though." He didn't want there to be anyone else, but that was stupid if he'd thrown out his armor. Quickly, he dismounted then helped his grandmother down.

"I'm looking forward to meeting both of them."

Trace strode to the door and knocked. Not hearing anyone, he knocked again. This time he distinctly heard a grunt. He opened the door and let his grandmother proceed him.

"You must be Uncle Joey." She took the man's hand and patted it before sitting down in the chair opposite him. His grandmother was an angel in his book.

He clapped his hand on Joey's shoulder as he came around to his front. "It's me, Trace. I brought you a little company. I hope you don't mind."

Joey rolled his eyes and opened his mouth.

"Is Whisper here?"

Joey jerked his head.

Trace looked at his grandma. "That means yes." He turned

back to Joey. "We need Whisper's help with a horse. If she agrees to come with me, my grandmother, her name is Annette, will stay here so you won't be alone."

Joey rolled his eyes again.

Trace chuckled. "I know what you mean. Everyone babies you. But if I were you, I'd milk it for all it's worth."

Joey's mouth opened again.

"We'll be fine, Trace. Go find Whisper and get back to that horse."

He nodded before turning to Joey. "See you later when I bring Whisper back. Cross your fingers she's willing to go, or you'll be seeing me a lot earlier."

Joey jerked his head and Trace left the trailer.

Now to find Whisper. The ATV was still under its cover so she had to be on foot. They had a rare rain last night, so he might have a chance of tracking her. Walking the perimeter, he found where she'd gone into the desert. Following her footprints, he kept an eye out for rattlers. This time of day they were generally sleeping and he wanted to keep it that way.

The area behind the trailer was less populated with Joshua trees. Instead, it had the typical prickly pear, saguaro, and jumping cholla cacti. But there were a lot of palo verde trees as well as large boulders. He saw the ATV path and as much as he wanted to discover where she went on the machine, it was more important that he find her.

He stopped on top of a boulder at the edge of a particularly rocky area, trying to find her tracks again. This could take all day. She could be miles from the trailer for all he knew. Then again, he couldn't see her leaving her uncle for too long. Climbing onto a very large boulder, he yelled, "Whisper!"

Shit, her name made yelling a contradiction. His voice didn't carry the consonants. He could fire off his gun, but he'd left it attached to Lightyear's saddle. He tried again, cupping his hands around his mouth. "Whisper!"

He listened, but his only response was silence. Damn, he needed to get her to Last Chance. His gut told him she could help and Mystique didn't have much time. He kept walking, trying to find any sign she might have stepped back down onto the desert floor.

Frustrated, he finally turned back the way he'd come to double-check the tracks he'd found. He halted. Now there were more tracks leading away from the boulder field. What the fuck? He would have seen them. She *was* out here and she was evading him.

He didn't have time for playing cat and mouse. Jumping down onto the desert floor, he stalked along the trail she left, a slow knot tightening in his belly at the time they were wasting. Growing more angry by the minute, he started to run, following the trail between trees and rocks, weaving in and out. Finally, he caught sight of her black ponytail as it disappeared down a small hill.

Gritting his jaw tight to keep from yelling, he ran full out, determination fueling his body. At the pounding of his boots on the hard ground, she finally turned and saw him.

"Whisper, stop."

She started to run.

He wasn't letting her get away. He kept after her, gaining until she was barely an arm's length away. He could have waited the two seconds it would take to grab her arm, but he was tired of wasting time. He threw his body toward her and toppled her to the ground, being careful to take the brunt of their fall.

"Let me go."

He rolled her beneath him. "I don't think so."

Chapter Three

Whisper's hat had come off and the sun glittered in her silver eyes. Her cheeks were flushed from her run, and he could feel her heart racing. He could also feel every womanly curve and that startled him. Some of those curves were bigger than he expected. "Why were you hiding from me?"

"Get off me."

"No, we need your help."

"I said get off me." She squirmed beneath him, her strength surprising.

"Whisper, listen to me. We have a horse that needs your help."

She stilled. "Why me? You have a vet."

Now how did she know that? Unless Dr. Jenna had talked about Last Chance. Is that how she found the spot for her trailer?

He shook his head. None of that mattered now. "Jenna doesn't know what to do. She says she can't find any reason why Mystique won't eat. I suggested you."

Her eyes widened. "Me? Why me?"

As his anger dissipated, his body started to react to the warm female beneath him. Not a good thing. He doubted Whisper would appreciate his interest in her body, so he moved off her and stood, offering his hand to help her up. "Because you said you liked animals better than people. Animals sense that."

She looked doubtful, but placed her hand in his. He held on as she gained her feet then reluctantly let her pull her hand away. That was strange in itself. She was not his type at all, especially since he'd sworn off down-on-their-luck women. She was tall and dark. His wife had been short and platinum blonde, though not a natural platinum.

Whisper brushed off her jeans, not saying a word. Then she bent over and picked up her hat. When she'd batted it a few times against her thigh, she placed it on her head. "I just want to be left alone."

The sincerity of her voice caused a tumult of reactions inside him. Understanding, disbelief, hurt. The last surprised him. "You mean you haven't become addicted to my charming smile and magnetic personality?" He couldn't help the touch of bitterness that crept into his question.

Her hat shaded her eyes as she contemplated him, probably wondering if he was serious or not.

"Listen, Whisper. You're this horse's only chance. We're desperate."

"You must be if you came for me. But I can't leave Joey for that long."

He could see she would throw out every possible excuse not to go. Time to rope her in. "I've brought my grandmother. She's already with him. Mystique has been starving for days. The only way they could get any nutrients into her was with a needle. If she doesn't eat on her own soon, we'll have to put her down."

"No." Whisper's quick denial seemed to startle her as well as him. She looked away, one hand burrowing into her front pocket. "Okay. But don't blame me if I can't help."

Relief and anticipation spread through him. "Thank you."

She nodded, but didn't say anything until they reached the trailer. "You brought a horse to get me?"

"What else would I bring?"

"An ATV, a truck."

He bent low and cupped his hands to help her mount. "Those wouldn't make it up the canyon wall."

She looked toward her ATV then back at him. "I've never ridden a horse."

He stood straight, staring at her. What the hell? Whisper was a study in contradictions. It would take a person a lifetime to figure her out. The challenge of that had his blood racing before he squashed his enthusiasm. The last woman he tried to "figure out" had cost him everything he had.

"It's not so important to have my help now, is it?" The bitterness in her voice had him softening.

"Your experience on a horse has nothing to do with saving Mystique. I was just surprised because most people out here know how to ride, but it's not a problem. All you have to do is place your foot into my hands and when I boost you up, throw your right leg over the saddle and sit. Do you think you can do that?"

"Oh, I can do that, but can you boost me? I'm pretty heavy." That she didn't say she was fat or put herself down, and instead just stated the facts, had him grinning.

"I think I can handle it. Ready?"

She ignored him and walked to Sadie's head. "If I'm too heavy for you, you just let us know, okay?"

The mare's ear twitched as she butted her nose against Whisper's shoulder. She walked back to him. "Okay, let's do this."

She made it sound like a major chore. He couldn't wait to see what she thought once they headed out.

With little effort, he helped her up into the saddle. "Nice view from up here."

He chuckled. Now why didn't it surprise him she wasn't scared? Mounting Lightyear, he walked him next to Sadie. "You will want to hold on to the saddle horn, especially as we descend. Sadie will follow Lightyear. Once we get to the bottom, I'll have you hold the reins and we can move a bit faster. Mystique needs you as fast as possible."

Never one for too many words, Whisper simply nodded and wrapped her hand around the saddle horn.

It made him want to know what she thought. That in itself was an oddity because most of the women he'd known always told him what they thought or felt unless they were just being stubborn, but Whisper simply preferred to keep to herself. As he started them toward the canyon wall, he grinned at the thought of the impression she would make on the rest of the family.

Whisper used one hand to pat the horse now and then as they approached the rim. The views from horseback were breathtaking. She'd never seen her little slice of heaven from this height and it reinforced for her that she'd picked the right spot.

The problem was Trace and his family. It had been just over twenty-four hours since she'd seen him last and he was already back. Despite her attempt to elude him, the damn desert floor had given her away. On the other hand, if they were going to put down a horse, she was glad he caught up with her.

Her body flushed as she remembered his weight on top of hers. She'd melted on contact, not something she was happy about, but she was a female and she wasn't immune to the hardness of his chest and the strength of his thighs. On one hand, she wanted what she dreamed about. On the other hand, the reality of the culmination was so disappointing.

Maybe she should try it. If she was able to help the horse Mystique, she could ask for sex in return. She was pleasing to look at and Uncle Joey had told her a long time ago that it was a rare man that didn't want sex with a pretty lady. Her uncle had never married nor had he brought home any of the women in his life. He always told her, she came first.

Her heart swelled with love. Uncle Joey was first in her life, too. Instead of being selfish, she'd ask for gingerbread ice cream for her uncle as payment. It was his favorite, and they only made it in Canterbury and only at this time of year.

As Sadie started to descend, she could tell the horse knew where to walk and Whisper placed her trust in the animal. At the bottom, after a few sliding steps on the treacherous shale, Sadie halted next to Trace.

"How are you doing?" He looked at her with concern.

"Fine."

His lips quirked up on one side as he shook his head. "I should have known you'd be comfortable on a horse. Take those reins in your hands so we can pick up the pace."

After a brief instruction, Whisper kicked Sadie into a lope. The movement of the horse at first felt strange, but after a few minutes she caught the rhythm. The urge to go faster rifled through her and she signaled Sadie to run.

"Whoohooo!" She loved the rush of the breeze against her face, and the fast gait of the horse beneath her made her feel like the god Apollo riding his chariot across the sky. Or at least what she figured he felt.

"Whisper!" Trace rode up beside her, a scowl on his face.

She smiled at him even as the wind took her hat and whisked it away. He looked stunned and fell back a bit, but she didn't care. She'd never felt so alive.

Looking back, she watched him spin Lightyear around, jump from the horse, grab her hat and jump back on. Now she understood the phrase "poetry in motion." Trace's movements were fluid, making everything look easy when she knew they required a lot of strength and skill.

He caught up to her within seconds and nudged Lightyear toward her, forcing Sadie to correct her direction a bit. She looked forward again. They were almost to a partially constructed building on a hill. "What's that?" She had to yell over the sound of the galloping horses.

Trace leaned over and pulled the reins from her hands, signaling the horse to slow, probably because they were getting close to people.

"That was amazing. Can we do it again on the way back?" She looked at him, the half-smile on his face too endearing. What would his lips feel like on her own?

"You really liked that, didn't you?" He handed her hat to her and she smacked it against her thigh to loosen the dirt, careful not to hit Sadie.

"That was the best experience I've ever had in my life. Thank you." She plopped her hat on her head.

He raised his brow. "Even better than sex?"

"Oh, by far." She reached down and patted Sadie on the side of her neck. "What a good girl you are. You are my new favorite animal."

"I thought I was." Trace's words caught her attention and she looked at him.

There was something behind the teasing words. His mouth said one thing but his eyes said another. He almost looked hurt or insulted. She couldn't decide. "You're a human. That's a whole different category."

She returned her gaze to the roughed-out road they traveled. "What was that big building being built on the hill?"

"That will be Lacey and Cole's house when it's done. I think they're just waiting for it to be finished so they can get married. That will be an interesting ceremony. My aunt Beverly never approved of Lacey."

Whisper had never seen anyone get married before. It would be nice to see Lacey get married. Lacey was a good person. If her husband-to-be's mother didn't like her, they shouldn't invite her. That would ruin what could be a wonderful day for Lacey. She hadn't missed how Lacey's eyes had lit up when she mentioned her fiancé, even while they were pinned down by the gunfire of the animal abuser.

She found herself getting anxious to see Lacey again, and Sacnite. Shit, what was the name Lacey called the horse? Something white. Snow? Ghost? Angel? Angel. That was it.

"You seem awfully deep in thought. Are you trying to figure out how to get the mare to eat?"

She snapped her head to the right, having completely forgotten Trace. Strange. People usually made her very uncomfortable. She never "forgot" they were around. "No. I won't know that until I sense her feelings."

Trace raised an eyebrow, but he didn't laugh or look doubtful. She let out her breath. Maybe he really did believe she could help. That encouraged her. She was used to people doubting her on every level.

"Here we are." Trace jumped down from his horse in one smooth movement, reminding her of a mountain lion who came by once in a while. Maybe that's why she was more comfortable around Trace. She could relate him to an animal.

He stood next to her horse and raised his hands. "Ready to come down?"

"Not really, but I guess I have to if I want to help." She took her feet out of the stirrups and leaned forward so she could swing her leg over the horse's rump.

"Whoa there." Trace's hand on her leg startled her. "Leave

this foot in the stirrup then swing one leg over and I'll help you down. Don't hit Sadie's rump."

She could do that. Putting her left foot back in the stirrup, she swung her leg extra high to avoid hitting Sadie but as she came around, she lost her balance and started to fall backward.

"Don't worry. I've got you."

She landed in Trace's arms, her left foot still attached to the horse. Shocked he could hold most of her weight, she quickly dislodged her foot.

She looked up at him. "Sorry."

He stared down at her, still holding her. His eyes turned dark and her heart started to tap hard like a woodpecker at a tree. He was so close she could see the long, dark lashes that outlined his eyes.

"Is that Whisper?" Lacey's voice came from the barn as she strode toward them.

Trace gently propped her up straight and she adjusted her hat, just to have something to do.

"It's so good to see you again." Lacey enveloped her in a big hug, despite the fact she was a good half foot shorter.

Whisper looked at Trace, but he just grinned. Hesitantly, she wrapped her arms around the woman and tapped her on the back. "Good to see you're still alive."

Lacey pulled back. "Only thanks to you."

"I don't know. You were doing pretty well on your own."

Lacey hooked her arm and started walking her toward the barn. "No way. I was a goner if you hadn't shown up. I actually aimed to kill that bastard and hit the ground three feet in front of him."

Whisper halted. "You tried to kill him?" A new respect for Lacey built.

Lacey scowled, a look Whisper hadn't seen before. "Dang right I did. He was going to shoot Cole."

Understanding dawned. Lacey was a sweetheart, but threaten those she loved, like her horse or her fiancé, and watch out. She let Lacey move her toward the barn.

When they stepped inside, she halted again. Jenna, the vet, stood next to a stall and a man leaned against the opposite one. From the scowl on his face, he wasn't happy. A hand on her shoulder had her turning her head.

"I understand you know Dr. Jenna. The brooding man over there with the baby in his arms is my brother, Logan. Don't mind him. He's in a perpetual bad mood. He doesn't get much sleep because his daughter is only six months old and likes to get up at all hours of the night."

She could feel Logan's anger simmering beneath the surface, but when he looked back down at his daughter, his whole demeanor changed for the better. She took in that observation and stored it for contemplation later. "Where's the horse?"

Lacey let go of her, walking to the vet and finally pointing to a stall. "This is Mystique. She and her two companions, Rogue and Storm were all starving. Rogue and Storm came first and they are eating, but the mare won't."

Whisper ignored the vet and Logan and moved to the stall where the horse stood facing the far wall. Opening the door, she went inside. She swallowed hard to keep the tears at bay as she got a close-up view of Mystique's ribs. Careful not to touch her, she moved to the mare's head.

Oh God. There was no spirit left in the body. Whisper straightened her shoulders, determined to find a way to understand the horse. She knelt on the ground before Mystique. She focused on the horse's eyes. Mystique's gaze remained down.

Whisper lay down, where the horse couldn't avoid seeing her. The deep-brown eyes were scared and something else. Whisper didn't breathe, holding the horse's gaze, and then a feeling of stark loneliness settled in her bones. Her eyes watered, the feeling too close to her heart for comfort.

She reached her hand up and touched the horse's nose. "I can help."

Slowly, she sat again, still watching Mystique. The horse's head remained down, but her gaze followed her. Just the tiniest show of curiosity, but it was a spark of life.

Hope built in her heart. "I'm going to stay with you until we get things right." She looked toward the stall door where Lacey waited patiently. "Where are Rogue and Storm?"

"We have them in the corral, outside."

Whispered nodded to show she understood. "I need to take her out there."

Lacey's brow furrowed. "Are you sure?"

"Yes." Ignoring Lacey, Whisper let her gaze return to Mystique. The horse continued to watch her. "We're going to see Storm and Rogue now."

The horse's ears twitched.

Whisper's confidence grew. "Storm and Rogue will be happy to see you again."

This time the horse's ears perked up.

She stood slowly. "You want to see Storm and Rogue?"

The horse continued to watch her, so she moved to the stall door. "Are you coming to see Storm and Rogue?"

Mystique turned around and Whisper opened the stall door.

Trace stepped forward with a halter. "I can put this on her."

She nodded but continued to talk to the horse. "Put this on so you can see Storm and Rogue."

Trace worked quickly then handed her the reins.

She never stopped talking to Mystique as she led the horse toward the corral, constantly mentioning Storm and Rogue. As they drew closer, Mystique's nostrils flared. When a weak whinny from the corral drifted to them, the mare lifted her head to look.

Whisper sensed the second Mystique recognized her friends. There was no pulling on the reins or answering sound, but there was a calmness in her walk, like someone coming home.

Trace met her at the gate and opened it to let them in and closed it behind them.

Immediately, Storm and Rogue walked over to greet Mystique. The mare trembled as she was welcomed.

Whisper turned to Trace. "Feed them all, now."

Jenna leaned on the corral fence. "The other two have eaten, they need to wait."

"No." Whisper looked at the vet. "Feed them all now. It doesn't have to be a lot."

Trace headed toward the barn. "I've got this."

Jenna ran after him, but Whisper returned her attention to the horses. Storm scratched Mystique's back with his teeth and the mare's head rose higher to return the favor. Rogue moved himself to be side by side with her.

Whisper's tension eased. Now that the mare was reunited with her friends, maybe she would eat.

Trace strode toward her carrying a bucket of grain. Again she was reminded of an animal, but not a mountain lion this time. Instead, his broadness reminded her of a black bear she'd once seen up north standing on his hind legs scratching his back against a tree trunk. Yet Trace's stride was all his, confident, strong, sexy.

She snapped her gaze back to the horses and her idea of asking him to have sex with her resurfaced. *No, gingerbread ice cream. Remember?*

Trace climbed the fence and dropped down inside the corral. He softened his landing by bending his knees, obviously not wanting to startle the horses. He moved to the tray that had been put out for them and emptied his bucket. "Come and get it." He grinned at her as he stepped aside.

Storm immediately moved, jostling Mystique. Rogue followed and Mystique, not wanting to be left alone, joined them. As soon as she saw the food, she lowered her head and ate with her friends, sandwiched between them.

Whisper sighed with relief even as Trace walked toward her. "You did it."

His look was full of pride and she felt her cheeks flush. She shrugged. "I guessed."

He shook his head. "No, I saw you in there. You understood her. Is that why your name is Whisper? Because you are a horse whisperer?"

She chuckled. "Not even close."

Trace stared at her a moment before his face softened. "I like the sound of your laugh."

She didn't know what she was supposed to say to that, so she kept her mouth closed.

His grin reappeared. "You have my curiosity piqued now. You must tell me how you got your name."

She leaned back against the fence, pleased by his attention. "It's not that exciting. I guess I was a loud child. My mom used to tell me to whisper to help me control the volume of my voice both inside and out. She said it so many times around my little friends that they started calling me Whisper. After my parents died, I begged Uncle Joey to let me change it. After many years, because he is one stubborn cuss, he finally gave in and at the age of thirteen I officially became Whisper Adams."

There was no reason to tell Trace that Joey allowed her to

change it in the hope that it would throw her relatives off her trail, but they eventually caught up to them…again.

"Joey told me your parents were gone. How old were you when they passed?"

"I was eight." That had been the worst day of her life. The day her life had changed forever. In a way, she was thankful because she'd learned how people really are.

"Shit. That's tough." He looked away, watching the horses. "I lost my dad when I was thirty and I thought that was hard." He looked back at her. "I can see now why you and your uncle have such a close bond."

She gazed into his eyes. They were the color of perfectly brewed tea. They definitely had her waking up. What would he do if she asked him for sex? Suddenly, the idea of rejection loomed large and she looked away. "I should get back to him."

"Right." He turned and opened the gate.

Lacey and Jenna were just leaving the barn. Lacey came up and gave her another hug. "You did it! I'm so glad you came. You have to stay for dinner."

Whisper warmed at Lacey's honest enthusiasm. "I can't. I need to feed my uncle."

"Oh right."

Jenna held out her hand. "Thank you. Now I know who to turn to when I get stumped. I always said there was more to an animal than just the mechanics. You proved me right."

"I hope she gets better." Whisper glanced over at the horses before turning to Trace. "Don't separate her from them until she's back to the weight she's supposed to be. Feed them as Dr. Jenna told you but feed them together. If you put them in the barn at night, be sure to have the other two across from her so she can see them."

Traced grinned. "Yes, ma'am."

At movement behind him, she looked past Trace to see his brother carrying his baby to the house. Though he cradled his child with care, she sensed a lot of anger and hurt in that man. She didn't like being near him and was glad he stayed away. She refocused on Trace. "Can we go?"

"Of course."

~~*~~

Trace smiled as he mounted Lightyear. He'd only been awake half an hour after a long night of thinking about Whisper when Lacey decided she had to invite her new best friend to the New Year's Eve party tomorrow night. Since he was the only one, besides his grandmother now, who knew where Whisper was camped, he was asked to play escort.

He had absolutely no problem with that. Whisper was a puzzle he just couldn't let remain unsolved. She acted like no other woman he'd ever met. Her lack of ambition alone was odd not to mention her preference for silence instead of talking. He wanted her to talk more, which had never been the case for him when it came to a woman.

It was curiosity that spurred him on. Though he no longer trusted his gut, it kept telling him she was exactly as she appeared, no hidden agenda. Also, it appeared she had no interest in him, which was good. They could be friends.

"Is it much farther?" Lacey crested the canyon rim and brought Angel up beside him.

He grinned. "Tired already, Blondie?"

She rolled her eyes at him. "Hardly. I still have a hundred items on my to-do list for tomorrow's party and I plan to complete every one before Cole gets home tomorrow morning."

"Have you two talked any more about Whisper staying here?"

Lacey shook her head. "No. Between the party, the new horses and his schedule at the fire station, we haven't had a minute together. But don't worry, I told Annette what Cole wanted to do and after her visit with Whisper's uncle, she's on our side."

"Wow, I never pegged you for the devious type."

She swatted him on the arm. "I'm not. I just know we owe a lot to Whisper and though Cole thinks it's the right thing to do to make her move, I know it's wrong. I just need to make him see that. You know how stubborn he can be about walking the straight and narrow. I need all the help I can get to make him see, in this case, the path to what's right is different than what he thought."

"I hope you can make him see the light because if he doesn't, he and I are going to have more than words."

Lacey stared at him. "Why would you care if she has to move?"

Good question. "Just wait and you'll see. You'd have to have a heart of stone to meet Joey and see what she's built and still force them to move."

"And we all know your heart is mush." She winked.

He shook his head and kicked Lightyear into a walk. He hated that she was right. He did have a soft spot that was as big and as weak as a newborn calf, especially with women. Family was one thing, but he needed to be a lot more distant with other women. More like Logan, but without the angry cloud.

By the time they arrived at Whisper's trailer, he'd convinced himself Whisper didn't need his help and could hold her own against Cole, especially with a gun. So he needed to keep his distance. Now that Lacey knew where Whisper lived, she could play guide to whoever else needed to come up here.

"Wow, this is a lot nicer than I expected." Lacey jumped down from Angel and wrapped the reins around a mesquite branch. "What a great spot." She turned around and took in the view.

Trace grudgingly agreed. Whisper and Joey had spectacular desert scenery. There were rock mountains on opposite sides with unique shapes carved upon them. On the south side was the Joshua tree forest they'd come through, a fascinating sight in itself and the west side was full of scrub brush and cacti with palo verde and mesquite trees thrown in for good measure for as far as the eye could see.

Swearing coming from inside the shed caught their attention just before a shapely butt covered in tight jeans appeared, backing out of the shed. From instinct, he ran over to help. "Here, I can do that for you."

Whisper dropped what she'd been pulling and snapped upright. "Where the hell did you come from?"

He smirked. "Last Chance Ranch, where else?"

She stepped back, shaking her head. "Why has my secluded spot suddenly become the trough at feeding time?"

He kicked himself for rushing to help. He'd startled her and now she was pissed and he couldn't blame her. And what happened to keeping his distance?

Lacey came to his rescue. "Whisper." She stepped right up to Whisper and gave her a hug.

Whisper scowled at him, and he shrugged. He was just the guide. Not his fault.

When Lacey was done, Whisper managed not to scowl, but he could tell she was still unhappy about their visit.

"So what are you doing here?" She addressed her question to Lacey.

Lacey smiled. "I asked Trace to show me where you lived, so I could invite you to my New Year's Eve party tomorrow night."

Chapter Four

W hisper coughed. "You're kidding, right?"

Lacey shook her head. "It's a very special party and I wouldn't even be alive to host it if you hadn't helped me on Christmas day."

Trace's already high opinion of Lacey rose another notch. The woman really knew how to get to people. If she couldn't get Cole to change his mind about Whisper living here, no one would. He might not have to bloody his cousin's pretty face after all.

"You don't know that." Oh, Whisper was pretty tough too. "You could very well have kept that piece of trash at bay long enough for your fiancé to rescue you."

Trace moved his gaze to Lacey, thoroughly enjoying the debate.

"Oh no, I would have run out of shot long before Cole showed up."

"But you could have started an avalanche of stone or something."

Lacey shook her head. "It really doesn't matter if you saved my life or not. The fact is, I met you and I like you and I really want my friends to be at this party."

"Friends?" That one-word question from Whisper had Trace sucking in his breath.

Why did he get the feeling the woman had never had a friend? He tried to steel himself against the sympathy that rushed through him, but it was hopeless.

Lacey pretended Whisper hadn't just revealed a heart-wrenching fact about herself. "Yes, friends. I really need my friends at this party because Cole's mother might show up and, well…" Lacey looked down as she paused.

Holy shit was Lacey good at this. He almost felt sorry for Whisper. She had no clue she was going to this party.

Lacey continued. "She doesn't like me. She thinks Cole can do better. That's why I need my friends there, you there. Basically, I need people who will keep me from telling the woman off."

Whisper's lips quirked upward just a bit and Trace felt a sudden yearning to see the woman actually smile or laugh fully or somehow show joy beyond a quirk of her lips or a small chuckle. She wasn't angry like Logan, just reserved and always wary. He wanted to know why.

"If you're looking for someone to hold you back, I'm not the one. I'm more likely to tell her off myself." It was clear Whisper thought she'd just won the debate.

Trace held his breath for Lacey's comeback.

Lacey's shoulders slumped. "But that's the other reason I need you there. I'm afraid that when she says something snide or nasty to me I'll be so hurt I'll run from the room crying."

Trace stood frozen. Sweet, innocent, *honest* Lacey was a master manipulator! He would never have believed it if he hadn't heard it with his own ears. He grinned. Cole had no idea what he was in for. At least Lacey loved his cousin, so the man was safe.

He glanced at Whisper and could see her wavering. He

would be so proud of her if she didn't cave in, but then it meant she wouldn't be at the party and he was absolutely sure the party would be much more interesting with her there.

He watched as she studied Lacey then she sighed. "No. I don't do parties."

Trace had to swallow his laughter at Lacey's shocked face. He wanted to cheer for Whisper, but that wouldn't go over well with either woman.

"Why not?"

Whisper shook her head. "I don't like people."

"But you like me, don't you?" Lacey was honestly hurt.

Whisper nodded.

Lacey pointed. "And you like Trace, right?"

He held his breath as Whisper's gaze moved to him. Her eyes revealed nothing and for a few moments she just stared at him. Finally, she nodded.

Shit, her answer was far more important to him than it should have been.

Lacey continued. "And you know Dr. Jenna. She'll be there."

Whisper caught on quickly. "Doesn't matter. I have to stay with Uncle Joey. You can't tell me you have someone in your family who would rather stay here with him than be at the party."

Lacey grinned. "Already thought of that. We'll bring Uncle Joey to stay the night at Last Chance. Logan hired a babysitter so she and Uncle Joey can watch over baby Charlotte."

Trace liked the way she'd phrased that. Uncle Joey may be an invalid, but his brain was far from a child.

Whisper's eyes widened before she glanced at the trailer.

Lacey pressed her advantage. "I'm sure your uncle would enjoy meeting more people. Please, Whisper. I really want you to come. It won't be the same if you're not there."

He couldn't keep quiet any longer. "I promise if at any time you feel uncomfortable and want to leave, I'll bring you back here."

Her gaze snapped to his again. "Okay, I'll go." She gave *him* her answer, but Lacey threw herself at Whisper, enveloping her in a hug. Trace raised his eyebrow and shrugged, but he was jealous of Lacey's freedom of expression. Why the hell couldn't he hug Whisper, too? And kiss her? And—shit.

Lacey broke away. "Thank you so much."

"I get to leave when I want." Whisper's voice was hard.

Lacey nodded enthusiastically. "Absolutely. Trace or Logan or—"

"Trace." Whisper was adamant. "Only Trace."

His chest swelled even as Lacey looked at him. "Of course. You know Trace the best. He can take you home whenever you're ready." She turned back to Whisper. "Now I'd like to meet Uncle Joey."

Whisper shrugged. She'd obviously decided there was no stopping Lacey once her mind was made up. "Sure. Go ahead." She held her arm out toward the trailer and Lacey strode toward it.

He fell into step next to Whisper. "She's a tough one to stand against."

Whisper looked at him. "But she has a good heart."

"What about me?" He had no idea why he'd asked, but he was curious what her answer might be.

"Jury's still out."

He stopped and laughed. The absolute blunt honesty of the woman enthralled him. "Fair enough." He waited where he was as Whisper spoke to Lacey before Lacey entered the trailer.

Whisper turned back to him. "You wanted to help. Come on."

He'd already forgotten he'd made the offer, but Whisper seemed to want to take advantage of him being there. Too bad she didn't want to take advantage of his body too.

His cock hardened at the thought. Was she as busty as he'd felt beneath her clothes? Her jeans today showed she had full hips and ass. The kind a man could hold on to when pumping in from behind.

"Are you gonna help or not?" Whisper stood by the shed door, frowning at him.

"Yes." He strode toward her, hoping the heat he felt in his body wasn't obvious. "What do you need?"

She pointed at a big-ass generator. "I need to get this out so I can see to fix the wheel."

"Wouldn't a flashlight or lantern inside the shed be easier?"

"If you don't want to help just say so."

"No, I do. It was a legitimate question."

She sighed heavily, and he could have sworn she muttered the word "people" under her breath. "There is no room in the shed to work on the generator. I'd rather pull this out than empty the shed."

Okay, she had a point. "No problem. Let me drag it out for you."

Whisper finally stepped back and allowed him access to the machine. She'd already moved it a couple feet to the edge of the doorway. Luckily, there was no lip on the floor. She'd obviously built the shed by hand and the concrete slab rose about an inch from the ground.

Grasping the handle of the generator, he pulled, succeeding in getting a quarter of the machine outside, but of course the axel for the broken wheel was at the back. Now he would have to lift it as well as pull.

The lack of a breeze had him heating up quickly. Taking

his bandana from his back pocket, he wiped the sweat from his brow before resettling his hat, then he anchored his feet and pulled again. Halfway there.

Again he took out his bandana and reapplied it. Shit, he'd be soaked in another thirty seconds. Without hesitation, he unbuttoned his shirt and whipped it off, throwing it on a bucket in the shed. He gripped the handles again, lifted and heaved.

His muscles strained as he determinedly dragged the generator the rest of the way out of the shed, even hauling it another foot across the desert floor. Taking his bandana from his pocket once again, he wiped his face then looked at Whisper in triumph.

Her eyes were wide as she stared at him. No, not at him, at his chest, and she licked her lips. The vision of her licking at his cock rose up before him and took his breath away.

Her cheeks were flushed, communicating her attraction.

He simply couldn't resist the pull she had on him and strode toward her. Her gaze didn't lift from his chest even as he halted less than a foot away. He took her hand and laid it on his pectoral. At her touch, his hot body shivered for an instant.

With his other hand he lifted her chin, forcing her gaze to connect with his. His breath caught at the raw, unadulterated desire in her gray eyes. His cock grew hard with need even as his gaze dropped to her full lips. He had to have her.

He lowered his head and pressed his lips against hers. Her mouth opened and his tongue slipped inside. Hers met his and they tangled, sending desire coursing through his blood. He moved his hand to the back of her head, coaxing her head to the side so he could deepen the kiss, explore every nuance of her taste.

At her moan, he released her hand and pulled her tight against him, pushing his hardened cock against her mons. Her arms wrapped around his neck and she pressed her breasts against his bare chest. His cock jerked at the pressure of her hardened nipples through her shirt.

The woman wore no bra.

His need burned hotter than he'd ever known. He wanted to take her now, on the ground if need be. He moved his hand from her head to between them, easing away an inch to touch the hard nipple against him.

Her moan was loud and uninhibited as her tongue released his and her head fell back. He kissed her jaw while his fingers played.

He had to touch her. Quickly, he left her nipple and unbuttoned one button, just enough so he could slide his hand inside and feel the hard nub of her other breast.

"Yes. More." Whisper's husky voice spurred him on.

He pinched the tightened nipple before rolling it between his thumb and fingers.

Her hand moved from around his neck and she unbuttoned three more buttons in quick succession. "Taste." She held her other breast up in offering to him.

Shit, there was no way he would pass that up. He lowered his head, still holding her at the waist as she arched back. He closed him mouth over her areola and nipple, inhaling her intoxicating scent. Sage and mint filled his nostrils as he sucked.

"Yes. More."

He sucked harder, eliciting a moan from the woman in his arms. He let up and encircled her hard nub with his tongue before taking the nipple between his teeth and moving his jaw back and forth.

Whisper's pelvis pressed determinedly against his cock and he used his free hand to pull the gun from her waistband. He stuck it in the back of his pants then filled the void in her jeans with his hand. He burrowed down to feel soft panties keeping him from his goal.

Slipping his fingers beneath the light material, he found what he sought and his balls tightened at how wet her folds were. He slipped a finger inside her slick opening.

"Oh shit." Whisper sank to the ground and he knelt with her, pushing his finger deeper.

Her hips pushed up to meet him, her sheath grasping his single digit. He pulled it out and began to push two inside her, but her channel was tight. His cock throbbed at the thought of how it would feel, but his brain resumed control. She was too tight. He stilled, not wanting to hurt her, yet not wanting to stop. He gave the nipple in his mouth one more lick and pulled his head up to look her in the face. Her eyes were closed, her cheeks flushed and her mouth slightly open.

Her nipples peeked between her open shirt and her full breasts beckoned him to continue. He stared at the hard nipples awaiting his attention.

"You want to plunge inside me now, right? You can."

His gaze snapped up to meet her open eyes and resigned face. Cold water wouldn't have worked better to cool his raging cock. Something was seriously wrong with this picture. "Do you want me to?"

She shrugged. "If you want."

Her answer was the complete antithesis of what her body had been telling him just moments before. "When was the last time you had sex?"

She lowered her brows. "A long time. Maybe a dozen years or so."

Shock and relief barreled through him, sending mixed signals to his heart. That was a hell of a long time and could explain her narrow passage, but that meant she wasn't a virgin, which relieved his conscience considerably.

Still, her reaction to his potential penetration was strange. She was no wimpy miss and she was always honest and blunt. Maybe he needed to be as well. "Do you like sex?"

Her lips formed a real smirk that caught him so off guard, he almost missed her answer.

"Most of it." She lifted his hand that had been down her pants and pressed it against her breast. "I love this and what you did with your fingers."

His mind raced. Twelve years ago she would have been maybe eighteen? Younger? She liked being felt up but it was clear penetration was something to be endured. Holy shit, she'd probably had sex with some pimple-faced boy who was like a rutting horse. It was just a guess, but if he was even half right, he couldn't take her like this.

His fingers froze where they had been stroking the side of her breast. *I have to make this right for her.*

Her hand encouraged him to continue stroking but the reality of where they were intruded. This was not the time or place to show her the wonders of sex. He smoothed his hand over her breast then clasped hers. "I want you, like this, but not here and not now. Not when Lacey can come out the door and find us like this."

"But you do want me?" Whisper didn't look him in the eye when she asked and his heart lurched.

He lifted her chin and forced her to look at him. "I do. I won't be happy until I have you completely." As the words left his mouth, their truth shook him, but he didn't break eye contact.

Whisper studied him, looking for sincerity, then she gave a quick nod and unwrapped herself from his arms. "Good."

He helped her to stand and turned away as she buttoned her shirt. He strode back to get his own when a hand on his waistband caught him by surprise. He spun, ripping his jeans from the grasp.

Whisper frowned at him. "You have Sal." She wrapped her arms around him and pulled the Glock from the back of his pants.

Shit, even that slight touch had his disappointed cock reacting.

She stuck the gun into the front of her jeans and then stared at his chest. "You better put your shirt back on."

"Right." He turned around again and somehow got his arms through the sleeves. He buttoned his shirt up slowly, needing a moment to let his body cool down again. Taking a deep breath and letting it out, he tucked in the ends of his shirt. Finally in control of his racing libido, he turned around to face her, but she wasn't there.

Noises coming from inside the shed as items were moved around made it plain where she was. Shit, how could the woman go from being sexually aroused to working on a generator that quickly?

He started to step around the open door when he heard the door to the trailer close.

"Trace?"

"Over here."

He stepped to the shed opening and found Whisper's ass, once more in the air as she bent over a bench to pull out the drawer on a tool chest. He whipped himself back around and strode toward Lacey. Whisper had him in more knots than a cowboy had boots.

"I'm ready to go. I just have to say goodbye to Whisper." Lacey breezed by him, heading for the shed.

Good. He was ready to go too. Too ready. He walked over to their horses and unlooped the reins. He waited, his stomach rolling like a tumbleweed across the desert. He wanted Whisper. The revelation was a little too unsettling.

He'd sworn off women, especially those not in the best financial circumstances, yet she never talked about needing money or wanting something she couldn't afford, like Yvonne used to. Then again, Whisper didn't talk at all. Maybe her parents had gone overboard with telling her to be quiet.

At that thought, anger tightened his gut. Shit, here he was getting angry on her behalf when he didn't even know if her parents had said anything of the sort. What the hell? "Lacey. Let's go."

The two women looked at him before Lacey gave Whisper another hug and walked toward him. "Okay, okay. Hold your horses. I was just giving her some last-minute instructions about the party."

He cupped his hands and helped her to mount then stuck his foot in Lightyear's stirrup. "What possible instructions could the woman need for a party?" He swung his leg over and settled in his saddle.

Lacey looked at him and winked. "I had to tell her what time you'd be picking her up for your date, of course."

Trace stared as Lacey urged Angel into a walk between the Joshua trees.

"Date?" He glanced over at Whisper to find her watching him. She was one fine-looking woman. The idea found a warm place in his chest. He'd be proud to have her on his arm for Blondie's party. Grinning, he winked at his "date" then urged Lightyear to follow Lacey.

~~*~~

Whisper pulled her good pair of black cowboy boots out from the back of her closet and sat on the bed. She hadn't worn them since the last time she and Joey were at the lawyer's office, before his first stroke. It had literally been years.

She moved her arm to wipe the dust off them with her sleeve, but stopped herself just in time. Her shiny off-white blouse wouldn't look so good with dirt all over it.

She must have told Joey she wasn't going a dozen times during the day and at least that many times told him she couldn't wait. She was well aware of why she couldn't wait.

Trace.

She didn't want to go because she would have to act like people expected her to act. She didn't do that well, but Lacey had promised she could leave whenever she wanted. Whether she left early or late, she'd be coming home alone. She hadn't been alone at home since Joey had his first stroke three years ago.

Her uncle looked forward to staying overnight on Last Chance Ranch. Before his strokes, he'd been social. Not a lot, but he had a handful of friends he'd do stuff with, like play chess, go to a movie, check out a new art exhibit.

She'd seen the change in him over the last few days. Between Trace, his grandmother, Annette, and Lacey, she could see Joey's mind racing and his energy level was way up. Last night he'd let his gingerbread ice cream half melt before she could get him to focus on it. That never happened. He didn't go to bed until almost ten o'clock and he was just going to the ranch to babysit.

She picked up her boots and brought them to the kitchen. She used a paper towel to dust them off then she sat in the chair opposite Uncle Joey as she tugged them on. "What do you know, they still fit."

He opened his mouth.

She returned the smile as she stood. "Okay, final inspection. How do I look?"

Joey scrutinized her outfit from her long jean skirt to her high neck, long-sleeve button-down silk blouse. She turned around so he could inspect her tight bun, though she'd pulled a few strands out near her ears so she didn't look like a strict school teacher or something.

When she turned back, the extra material at the bottom of the skirt swirled a bit. It was kind of fun. "So? What's the verdict?"

Her uncle closed his eyes and took a deep breath before he grunted.

"That good?" Her feminine side trilled at his compliment. Because the blouse was off white, she'd worn a chemise underneath. By rights she should wear a bra, but she hadn't owned one since she was sixteen.

Joey jerked his head.

She sat down. "Thank you." She gazed at him, loving him for all he had done for her. It just wasn't fair he'd been dealt so many strokes. "You know you mean more to me than anyone."

Her uncle rolled his eyes and grunted. "Okay, so that's not saying much. How about this? I love you and I will never, ever leave you."

Joey closed his eyes and opened them.

She clasped his hand in hers and squeezed. "You know, you look pretty good yourself tonight. I hope you're not planning to pick up the other babysitter."

Joey grunted and she let go of his hand. "I'm just saying."

She looked at the clock in the kitchen. Trace would arrive any minute if Lacey had given him the right directions to the dirt road her ATV had created. At the possibility that he couldn't find her trailer via his truck, she looked out the window, suddenly wanting desperately to go to the party.

"I'm going to take a quick walk around the trailer just to make sure everything's okay."

Joey grunted.

"I know, I know. I'll be careful of my clothes." She grabbed up the blue wool cape she'd bought from a Native American woman at a craft fair that had come through town a couple years ago. It had designs on it she liked, but this would be the first time she wore it. Desert dust wasn't kind to good clothes.

Throwing the cape on, she attached the hook and eye clasps and grabbed up her flashlight before heading outside. The sky was almost dark, but on this last day of the year, night always came early.

She walked around the trailer, not really looking for anything in particular. It wasn't as if she needed to lock things up when the only people who knew she lived out here were Trace and his relatives.

The air was crisp already. She was pretty sure they'd have a frost tonight. At least she'd repaired the wheel on the generator yesterday. That particular machine would be keeping the trailer warm tonight for when she returned home.

Finishing her stroll, she meandered out toward her ATV road. Looking down it, a flash of light caught her attention as it bounced off a saguaro cactus in the distance. Her heartbeat doubled. Trace was coming. Turning, she strode back to the trailer.

She needed to get Joey's coat on before Trace arrived. She'd pulled the wheelchair out of the shed earlier, and it waited near the door outside. Would Trace carry Joey out or should she get him out? She always did it by herself when he had a doctor's appointment.

As she reached for the door, headlights blinded her and she covered her eyes. The truck stopped and the lights were turned off. Suddenly, she felt like a rabbit caught in a snare. What if it wasn't Trace? What if it was one of her relatives? Shit. She was so anxious about tonight, she hadn't even taken Sal outside with her for protection.

"Whisper?" At the sound of Trace's voice, she relaxed, but then a buzzing in her stomach started as he came into the meager light of the trailer's windows.

Her heart skipped a beat at the sight of him.

Chapter Five

Trace strode toward her in a white button-down collared shirt and silver eagle bolo tie. His broad shoulders were accented by the black sport coat he wore with swirling blue embroidery that was thin at the button and wide at each shoulder. New blue jeans, shiny black cowboy boots and a black hat that almost covered his short brown hair completed his ensemble.

She expected him to stop and say howdy or something, but he didn't. He stepped right up to her, took her in his arms and kissed her.

Whisper grasped his waist as his tongue dove between her lips and blazed a trail of desire from her mouth all the way down to between her thighs, leaving her breathless.

When he finally pulled his lips from hers, he kept his arms about her and just stared, his face unreadable, but his breathing as rapid as hers.

"Good evening, Miss Adams."

She smirked. "A very good evening it is, Mr. Williams."

He grinned, his white teeth flashing in the trailer's lights. He stepped back. "Let me see."

She put her arms out. "See."

He chuckled. "No. You must do the obligatory turn around.

All I saw in the headlights was a sophisticated woman. I need to see if my eyes are playing tricks on me."

"Really?" She waited for him to say no, but he just stood there with his eyebrows raised in expectation. "Well, strip me naked and throw me in a lava pit."

He chuckled but twirled his finger at her.

She turned her back on him and looked over her shoulder. "Happy?"

He shook his head, stepped up behind her and encircled her waist with his arms. He inhaled slowly, his nose against her neck. "Hmm, you smell good."

She did take a shower. It was a party after all. She didn't smell the scent of her soap. She could only smell the spicy musk from his aftershave and feel how smooth his chin was against hers.

He squeezed her waist. "You feel good too."

He felt good to her, especially with his body flush against her back.

His lips found her neck beneath her hairline and he kissed her. After nibbling his way up to her ear, he pulled back. "You taste good too."

The lines from *Little Red Riding Hood* flitted through her mind and she laughed. "The better to eat you, my dear."

Trace's hold went slack, so she stepped away and faced him. He had a strange gleam in his eye and his smile wasn't quite full. "Trace?"

He shook his head as if to clear it. "Sorry, got a little sidetracked there. Is Uncle Joey ready?"

"Yes." She picked up her skirts and strode toward the door. "Let me just bring him out."

His hand on her shoulder, held her back. "Whoa there, cowgirl. That's a man's job."

She raised one eyebrow. "And who do you think carries him out here every time he needs to go to an appointment?"

Trace's smile faltered for a moment before he ushered her aside. "That may be, but you are not dressed for carting a grown man around."

She was about to point out that he wasn't dressed for it either, but it wouldn't do any good, so she waved him inside.

As she held the door open, she listened to him talk to her uncle. If there was one thing she'd have to admit, it was that every one of Trace's relatives had treated Joey with respect. She appreciated that. Others in the past didn't, which was one of the reasons she'd left the last mobile park down in Tucson. Uncle Joey missed the company, but too many of their neighbors made fun of him. Even those who were kind treated him like he was a baby. They just didn't get it.

"Here we are." Trace came out of the trailer holding Joey.

She let the door close and held on to the wheelchair so he could put Joey down.

Trace turned away from her. "It's not that far. Just open the passenger door."

She walked over to the truck and did as he asked. After settling Joey in the middle of the front seat and buckling him in, Trace held the door for her.

Taking her hand, he helped her up and waited for her to pull in the excess jean material of her skirt before he closed the door. She had to admit, he was quite the gentleman. Too bad she wasn't a lady.

She watched in the side-view mirror as Trace strode to the wheelchair and rolled it to the back of the truck before lifting it into the bed. The man moved with ease, much like his personality. After securing the wheelchair, he closed the tailgate then jumped into his seat behind the wheel. "Everyone ready?"

Joey jerked his head and she nodded.

Trace turned the truck around and followed the well-worn path back to town. It was definitely the long way around to Last Chance Ranch and she preferred riding over the canyon rim and through the valley on Sadie, but that could get treacherous at night between holes in the ground and snakes.

She liked the name of the ranch. In a way it fit her and Joey. It was their last chance for peace and tranquility. She'd tried living under the radar, but it appeared that "off the grid" was the only way to stay hidden and still have a life. "Why is it called Last Chance Ranch?"

"Oh, I thought you'd fallen asleep on me over there, you were so quiet." Trace elbowed Joey and he grunted, his mouth open.

She didn't mind. She was pleased that Joey was so excited. "That doesn't answer my question." She frowned at him, but he kept his eyes on the highway.

"Originally, it was because at a young age, my grandparents thought themselves getting up in their years."

"How old?"

He glanced at her and Joey. "Thirty."

Joey grunted.

She stared at him in surprise. "I agree with Joey. That's not old. Hell, that's my age now."

"I was wondering about that." Trace didn't look at her but didn't say anything else either.

"How old are you?"

"I'm thirty-two." His tone was bitter as if being that age was worthless.

"Why is that bad?"

"Because just a year ago I had accomplished so much. I owned a horse breeding ranch, my clients were happy, I could afford anything I wanted…except as it turned out, my wife."

Whisper's heart froze in her chest. She could barely get the words past her lips. "You're married?"

His laugh was more like a bark. "Not for long. Yvonne filed for divorce once she figured out how she could get everything I'd worked so hard for. I'm expecting the final court hearing any day. So far, it looks like I'm the big loser in this deal."

Ah, so that was why he was bitter. It made sense now. "So you came to Last Chance because it was your last resort?"

He chuckled, his good humor restored. "Something like that, though I use to spend half my summers out here as a child with my brother, Logan, and my cousins Cole and Dillion. So moving here was almost like coming home."

He held one arm in front of Joey as he made the sharp left turn onto a dirt road. It was so natural, he probably didn't realize he did it.

"So why is it called Last Chance if your grandparents were so young?"

"You're like a squirrel on a bird feeder, persistent. Like I said, they thought they were on the verge of being too old to start a cattle ranch, so they figured it was their 'last chance' to put down roots. Of course, back then, people didn't move around as much as they do now."

That was true. "I think the name fits well now because of the horses you take in."

"In many cases, we *are* their last chance, but luckily we are able to place a lot of them either with families or at trail riding ranches. We even have four we placed at Poker Flat nudist resort." He winked at her. "Can you imagine riding a horse naked?"

"That sounds like heaven. Is this resort nearby?"

He lowered his brows before holding his arm out in front of her uncle as he turned into the drive and under the sign of the ranch. "That's where Lacey works. Didn't she tell you that?"

"When I met Lacey we were being shot at by Sca—Angel's former owner, so no, it didn't come up."

He parked the truck next to a dozen other vehicles. "Many people coming tonight work at Poker Flat. Lacey also arranged with her boss to have rooms there for the people who came up from her hometown of Orson. No one will want to make the two-hour drive back there. Lacey has one of the security guards running a shuttle to the resort to keep everyone safe."

"So the resort is close?"

Trace stared at her. "Why? Do you want to go there?"

"If I can ride a horse like Sadie naked, then yes."

He shook his head. "I'm pretty sure the best you're allowed to do there is walk the horse." He grinned. "But I'd be happy to take you there sometime if you want to try it."

She liked the idea of the two of them riding naked. Trace was so in tune with his mount, she could almost see him naked on Lightyear, his solid thighs gripping the horse's sides as his abdominals worked like waves while he moved with his horse. Yes, she wanted to do that.

She turned to tell him so, but Trace jumped out of the truck and came to her door. She could get down just fine by herself, but she kept her mouth shut and allowed him to help her out. He was a gentleman, so she had to let him do what he needed to do.

He moved to the back of the truck and she leaned in to unbuckle Joey's seatbelt. "You're going to stay here in the big house, but don't be getting any ideas about fancy living or nothing."

Joey rolled his eyes and grunted.

"Yeah, you say that now, but just wait until you get into that cushy bed."

Trace rolled the wheelchair to where she stood.

"He needs his shoulders and head lifted about four inches higher than the rest of him at night. It helps him sleep better."

Trace leaned in and lifted Uncle Joey out of the front seat and set him in the chair. "Lacey already made arrangements for him to sleep in our grandparents bed because it's adjustable. They are going to take my room and use my bed and old Billy's bed for tonight. Billy is staying at Poker Flat. It's a big bed shuffle game."

"Where will you sleep?"

He shrugged. "I get the downstairs couch, but don't worry, it's plenty big. I've slept on it before."

She made sure Joey's feet were up on the foot rest and started to wheel him toward the house.

"Here, let me." Trace took the handles of the wheelchair from her.

She walked with him, unused to doing nothing. Joey was her responsibility. At the three steps to the porch, Trace turned the wheelchair around and pulled Joey up backward like a pro. It was another piece of information about Trace that she stored in the back of her mind for further contemplation at a later time.

Once they had Joey settled with the babysitter and baby Charlotte, they walked back to the truck. Just as Trace opened the door to the cab, a car drove into the ranch and stopped next to them.

"Hey good-lookin', is this the way to the party?"

Trace tipped his hat. "Yes it is, miss."

The sexy Hispanic woman looked Trace up and down. "I certainly hope you're coming too."

He chuckled, the damn flirt. "Yes, I am."

"Save a dance for me, cowboy." The woman waved and continued down the road toward Lacey and Cole's construction site.

Whisper didn't like anything about the woman. Couldn't she see Trace was with her? Hell, she'd learn to dance every song just to keep that lady away from Trace.

Trace caught her attention. "Up you go." After she was seated, he closed the door.

She waited for him to get in. "Who was that?"

"I'm not one hundred percent sure, but from her looks and the way she talked, I'm guessing that's Lacey's good friend Adriana, the bartender from Poker Flat."

"She's a friend of Lacey's?"

Trace chuckled even as he started the engine. "Yes. Hard to believe, isn't it?"

"I don't like the way she talked to you."

Trace leaned toward her. "Why? Are you jealous?"

Whisper thought about it a moment. "Yes."

His eyes widened. Then a seductive grin lifted the corners of his mouth. "I like that."

"You like that I'm mad that this Adriana flirted with you?"

"Yes."

She stared at him. "You're not making sense."

He snaked one hand behind her neck and pulled her closer, their noses almost touching. "Yes, I am. I like that you're mad at Adriana because that means you think of me as yours just like I think of you as mine."

He didn't let her respond. Instead he brought his lips to hers and kissed her, his tongue searching her mouth even as his other hand came up to cup her breast, his thumb rubbing back and forth across her nipple.

She grasped his shoulder and moaned at the pleasure coursing through her body and down to her vagina. She tried to end the kiss, but his hand on her neck refused to allow her to back away and she found his tongue pumping into her mouth as she melted against him.

Finally, he released her and sat up behind the steering wheel again.

She lay against the seat a moment while he lowered the windows.

"It's suddenly a little hot in here." He glanced back at her and smirked. "Ready to meet the family?"

She shook her head even as she raised herself to a sitting position. The thought of all the people who would be at this party had her blood cooling quickly. "I get to leave when I want. Remember that."

His face lost its grin as he pulled the truck onto the dirt road that led to Lacey and Cole's partially constructed house. "You can count on me."

She had to admit, she felt better knowing Trace would take her home as soon as she wanted to go. She planned to watch the party from a quiet corner, unless of course that Adriana woman decided to dance with Trace. Shit, she'd have to go everywhere with him. On one hand, that made her nervous, but on the other hand, she certainly wouldn't mind being next to him all night.

He smelled good and looked better than handsome. She was damn proud to be walking into this party with him.

Within a couple minutes, they were parked, out of the vehicle, and headed toward the bright light seeping through the plastic-covered holes that would someday be filled with windows. The subtle sound of a base beat broke the quiet night and the murmur of voices grew louder as they approached.

She found herself hesitating and Trace halted only three

yards from the door. He grasped her hand and stepped in front of her. "Have I told you how beautiful you look tonight?"

She flushed with pleasure. "No."

He smiled and his free hand came up to stroke her cheek. "That's terrible because I think you look stunning tonight. I'm very happy you accepted Lacey's invitation to be my date."

Date? She hadn't had a date in forever. She was sixteen when she'd gone to a pizza place and had pizza with her first boyfriend. She barely finished her dinner before he was dragging her out behind the building to kiss her and suck on her tits. He didn't do nearly as good a job as Trace.

She pressed his hand against her cheek, the feeling new and strange but very enjoyable, then she turned her face and kissed his palm. It was rough against her lips. She liked that he was rough and hard.

Trace lost his smile. "If you keep doing that we'll never make it to this party."

Shit, he didn't like it. She dropped his hand. "I'm sorry."

He grasped her hand in his again. "Don't be sorry. I loved it."

She couldn't tell if he was simply humoring her. It was too dark. "Really?"

He licked her palm then trailed his tongue between two fingers.

A shiver raced from her hand to her heart. "Okay, okay. I believe you."

He laughed, his white teeth gleaming. "I can't wait to introduce you to everyone."

She stiffened as panic swept through her. *If you can't say anything nice, don't say anything at all.* Her mother's words from so long ago raced through her mind and she latched on to them as they flew by. She could do this. She wasn't afraid of these people. It's not like they were her relatives.

"Your face is wonderful to watch, Whisper. Are you ready?" Trace gave her hand a reassuring squeeze.

She nodded and he hooked her arm in his.

"Then let's go party this year away."

~~*~~

Trace couldn't believe how much he was enjoying Lacey's party. A party was a party, but to experience it with Whisper was proving to be a joy in and of itself. After introducing her to someone, he took time for them to find a quiet corner and let her digest what she'd learned. Her questions were fascinating and her observations spot-on.

He led her once again to a less-populated area of the giant room. He had to admit Lacey, his grandmother and Cole had worked magic. The entire construction site now looked like a wedding bower or even heaven. He wasn't sure which. There was plenty of room for dancing and eating, and the food and alcohol flowed, literally. There was a chocolate fountain and a gingerbread village with a marshmallow river running through it.

Whisper took another sip of champagne; a choice of drink he hadn't expected from her. She was beyond intriguing. "Don't drink too much of that. We still have the champagne toast at midnight."

She looked at him as if he'd just told her the world was flat. He chuckled. He'd never had this much fun at his own parties. Maybe it was the company.

"I like Kendra." He could listen to Whisper's low, husky voice all night and not grow tired of it.

He glanced at the couple he'd just introduced her to, the owners of Poker Flat Nudist Resort. "Hmm, I found Kendra difficult to read. Then again, this is the first time I've met her.

Her boyfriend, Wade, I know because he's been here to look at horses. He's thinking about buying a couple more."

"That's why you told him about Storm, Rogue and Mystique?"

He nodded. Whisper would never refer to horses as just horses. To her, each was worthy of their own individuality. "Yes. My guess is, based on what you figured out, those three can never be separated or Mystique will suffer. Wade understands. Two of his horses, Sage and Daisy, are like that in a way. Sage won't budge without Daisy."

Whisper gave a small smile proving she had finally begun to relax a bit. "I'm glad your cousin is careful about who he gives his horses to." She pointed to his aunt. "I would never let her have a horse. She would ride it into the ground if it suited her. She is all about herself. See?"

He grasped her hand in an effort to avoid her drawing attention and watched as his aunt Beverly pulled a young, obviously wealthy, young woman over to talk to Cole, who was dressed in a formal western tux much like one Trace used to own. His curiosity was piqued by Whisper's observation. "How do you know that?"

She shrugged. "By watching her. When she gets into a conversation, she dominates it, demanding everyone's attention. After she leaves, you can see the people sigh in relief. It's like a twister came by and they are happy to have made it through without damage."

Trace laughed, drawing a bit more attention toward them than Whisper was comfortable with. At least that was his assumption based on the frown she gave him. "You are a genius."

"No, I'm not. My IQ isn't that high."

This time he stifled his laugh before it came out, but he

couldn't help his wide smile. "As a matter of fact, that woman you described so well is Cole's mother."

Whisper's gaze left him and went back to his aunt. "Why is she forcing Cole to talk to that woman when Lacey is his fiancée, or does she think Cole would leave Lacey that easily?"

Trace nodded. "That's what she thinks."

Whisper shook her head. "Cole would never leave Lacey. If he did, he wouldn't last long."

Trace's blood chilled at her statement. "What do you mean?"

"She's his whole world. He'd give up everything for her, not that Lacey would ask him to. It's so obvious."

He frowned. He would have done the same for Yvonne and apparently he *had* given up everything, but he was still alive. In fact, he never felt more alive than when he was with Whisper. Still, it rankled to be fleeced when his own motives had been honorable.

Maybe, as Cole once said, he was lucky to be free of the Ice Queen.

He studied Whisper as she watched the crowd. Her expressions were open and honest and nothing got past her.

She made to point again, but he still had her hand so she gestured with her glass. "Who's that over there getting a drink at the bar? The one with the black hair and brown cowboy hat?"

He looked to where she indicated. "That's my cousin Dillion. He's Cole's younger brother. He helps run Morning Creek Ranch, his parents' place. Cole doesn't mind that he handles the homestead. Cole is very happy here."

She looked back to his aunt Beverley. "That woman is barking up the wrong tree."

"Excuse me?"

Whisper shrugged and took another sip of champagne.

He couldn't help watching her lips on the rim of the glass. He loved the taste of her lips and her tongue. She wasn't shy at all, despite her lack of extensive experience. Maybe her observations of animals had her accepting how sex worked.

He froze in mid-swallow of his beer. Is that why she looked at penetration as something to be accepted? Had she ever had an orgasm?

His blood raced at the thought that he could be her first in all ways that counted. Shit, was it midnight yet? He'd half hoped Whisper would want to go home early, but he couldn't deny her this opportunity. It was good for her to socialize with people a little.

When he finally took his eyes from Whisper's lips, he silently groaned. "Uh-oh. Here comes Cole's mom and that poor woman she is dragging about with her. Aunt Beverly was probably rejected by Cole and is looking for someone else to match her up with. Take my arm. Please."

Whisper widened her eyes before she gave him that half smile that started his heart racing before she took his arm. "Do you want me to bat my eyelashes, too?"

He chuckled. "No, but if it looks bad, a kiss couldn't hurt." Actually, a kiss on his cheek might just do the trick.

His aunt stopped in front of him. "Trace, we haven't had a chance to meet your friend here." Beverly gave a short nod to Whisper before focusing on him.

He hated that she called Whisper a friend. He wanted her to be more than that. "Aunt Beverly, this is my date, Whisper Adams."

Beverly spared Whisper a brief nod before presenting Hailey. "Trace, I'd like you to meet Hailey Kahnes. You remember the Kahnes family, don't you? They lived in the next town over from your parents' ranch."

He smiled politely. "Nice to meet you, Hailey. This is Whisper, my girlfriend."

Hailey looked relieved at his pronouncement and turned toward Whisper. "Lacey told us how you saved her life. She was very lucky to find you."

Trace watched Whisper shrug. "Fate."

"What high school did you attend?"

"I didn't. I was home schooled." Whisper appeared proud of that fact. It fit a couple of her puzzle pieces together for him. She had an unusual repertoire of knowledge, which was probably due to Uncle Joey's interests.

But his aunt sniffed, clearly unimpressed. His body tensed. He'd never had the urge to smack a woman, but at that moment he had to clench his fist to keep from knocking some sense into his aunt.

Hailey shook her head. "That's not it then. Have we met before? You look familiar for some reason."

Whisper's face drained of color and Trace wrapped his arm around her waist to steady her. "I doubt it. She's local."

Hailey nodded, but wasn't convinced.

Beverly gave a tiny laugh, the fake high-society kind. "Oh, I doubt you know her, Hailey. Lacey tells me she lives in a trailer in the desert near this ranch. Hardly the same social circles."

Trace felt Whisper stiffen, but before he could defend her, Hailey nodded, leaned in and whispered, "She has no clue what circles I can ride in." She winked at Whisper and looped her arm in his aunt's. "So tell me, Beverley, who is that dashing looking man conferring with your mother? Perhaps you could introduce us."

Beverly quickly forgot about them and ushered Hailey off to meet Logan. Trace grinned. Good luck with that.

Hailey glanced back at Whisper once his aunt took over the

conversation. She really thought she knew Whisper and Whisper was as stiff as a board. What was she afraid of?

"Hey, if you can't relax, I may just have to take you out on the dance floor to loosen you up."

Whisper's gaze shifted to the dancers who were two-stepping around the floor and her arm tightened on his. "Shit. Here comes that Adriana woman."

He caught sight of the bartender from Poker Flat and grinned at Whisper's reaction. There was something about a jealous woman that set a man's pride up another notch.

Adriana sauntered toward them, her curvy body not hidden at all in the tight red minidress with spaghetti straps. He'd heard from Cole that the woman had a lot of sexual experience. It didn't surprise him, considering how hot she was.

When she was less than twelve feet away, his vision was suddenly blocked by Whisper's face. "Time for that kiss."

The second her lips touched his and her arms wrapped around his neck, he was lost. Her tongue dove into his mouth and he pulled her close, loving how free she was with her desire.

"Ahem. I don't mean to interrupt, but you're drawing an audience. Midnight is still thirty minutes away." The sultry voice took him off guard until he registered the meaning of the words.

Trace lifted his head and flushed at the dozen or so people who had turned around to watch him and Whisper. He kept his voice low. "Whisper, you need to let go. People are watching."

She released him and turned to meet everyone's stare then shrugged. "So?"

Adriana's laugh finally drew their attention. "Oh, I like you. Hi, my name is Adriana. I'm a good friend of Lacey's. She told me you're Whisper, another good friend of hers." Adriana held out her hand.

Whisper shook, but didn't say anything.

Adriana glanced from Whisper to him. "Well howdy, cowboy. I didn't realize you were taken." She sighed heavily. "Seems all the good ones are." She winked at Whisper, who continued in her silence.

Adriana swept her gaze over his girlfriend. "You look beautiful. I envy you your class."

Whisper's eyes widened then turned to slits. "What do you want?"

Adriana laughed again. "Oh, I do like you. A woman after my own heart. Tell it like you see it. To set your mind at rest, I'm not interested in your cowboy and—"

"His name is Trace."

Adriana nodded. "I'm sorry. We haven't been introduced. Hello, Trace."

He nodded once, not willing to delay the woman's explanation.

"I'm more interested in you, Whisper. I don't like people threatening my friends and Lacey told me what you did for her when she was pinned down by that piece of trash, Norton. I also like a woman who can hold her own. I've had to myself a time or two."

Whisper's tension eased a bit. "You say you like people to tell it like it is. Tell me then, when is the wedding going to start?"

Chapter Six

Trace's heart lurched in confusion. "Wedding?"

Adriana's eyes rounded before she adjusted her countenance. "Why do you ask about a wedding?"

Whisper appeared insulted. "Really? Let's see, the room is decorated in white, complete with white balloons and doves. Lacey is wearing a long white gown and both Cole and his brother Dillion are wearing tuxes. They each have a boutonniere and you have a corsage. Both families are represented as well as close friends, and I heard that person over there say he was a justice of the peace."

Trace looked at every person she mentioned then stared at her.

Adriana also looked at her, eyes wide. She leaned in. "Shh, it's going to be a surprise. Right after the New Year. No one knows but the specific people you mentioned."

Trace grinned. He had to hand it to Lacey. She hadn't said a word about it and she talked a lot. Not like Whisper, whose longest discourse all night had been her analysis of the surprise wedding.

"I won't say anything." She gave him a stern look as if he would. "At least I know how long I have to stay here."

"Aren't you having fun?" Adriana cocked her head in his direction.

Whisper gave her signature smirk. "I think I'll have more fun after the party."

Adriana laughed and Trace's balls reacted. Whisper just told him she wanted sex. Shit, he'd leave now, but she was right. Now that they knew there would be a wedding, they had to stay. Of course, everyone else would stay until the midnight countdown. Even his grandparents were still up and it was getting close to the end of the year.

"Trace, it was nice to meet you. I just hope you have the stamina for this one." Adriana winked and sauntered off, flirting herself into a dance with Dillion.

He turned toward Whisper, loosely wrapping his arms around her waist, not caring what anyone thought. "I think we need to have your IQ checked. I'm more convinced now than before that you're a genius."

She looped her hands around his neck. "Nope, I'm short one point."

Holy hell, he couldn't catch his balance with this woman. Maybe he could even the playing field. "Want to dance?"

She stiffened in his arms. "I don't know how."

"The only thing different from dancing and what we're doing is shifting your weight from one leg to the other."

She looked askance at him. "That's not what I see other people doing."

"Just wait. If I don't miss my guess, the next song will be a slow song."

They stood still, listening to the country song end. Another song started. It was slow as he predicted. "Okay, now I want you to watch my cousin, Dillion. See how he's moving with Adriana?"

She nodded.

"Think you can do that?"

She hesitated, but finally nodded again.

Whisper closed her eyes as she leaned her face against Trace's shoulder like she'd seen other women do with their partners. Back when she and Uncle Joey were still on the grid, she'd watched television shows and movies where people danced. It always fascinated her how everyone could move the same, but here that wasn't the case. Some people weren't even moving to the beat.

She let her body meld to Trace's, catching his rhythm and following him, much like she caught Sadie's rhythm and adjusted her movement to the horse's stride. He slowly rocked her into the crowd, but no one else existed in their world.

She saw a hand touch Trace's other shoulder and he turned them toward it.

"May I cut in?" Logan stood there, his body radiating irritation.

Trace squeezed her tighter. "No."

"Excuse me, little brother, but that's not polite."

Trace sighed and loosened his hold. "Just for a few minutes. Understand?"

Logan nodded. "Sure."

Whisper was wrapped in Logan's arms within seconds before she even had a chance to voice her opinion. "What do you want?"

"I just wanted to talk to you." Logan was as stiff as she was.

"Then talk."

He opened his mouth then closed it.

"Just spit it out. No need to be polite around me."

One of his eyebrows rose in response. "Okay. How much has Trace told you about his wife?"

She shrugged. "Not much. From what he said, I understand the divorce is not final yet. From what he hasn't said, I've figured out she is taking his ranch, his horses and his bank accounts. I'm not sure he's decided yet if she took his heart as well. I think his pride is hurt that a woman stole everything he worked for right out from under his nose, but I'd bet his heart is bruised, not broken."

Logan stopped dancing and stared at her. "Damn, you're scary."

An old feeling of inadequacy started to rise, but she stomped it down. "I've heard that before. Is that it?"

Logan started the rhythmic rocking again. "Not yet. I just want you to know that just because Trace doesn't have any money left to his name, doesn't mean he can't make some. He's done it once and he can do it again."

"Why would I care if he had money?"

Logan looked uncomfortable for the first time. "I'm just saying if you decided to have a long-term relationship with him, he would find a way to take care of you."

"Listen, Jack. I don't need anyone to take care of me. Uncle Joey did it until I was eighteen and I've been taking care of myself *and* him since I turned twenty-two."

"Fine. Just don't go breaking my brother's heart or I'll find you."

Whisper couldn't help smirking. "I've had people more determined than you give up trying to find me. If I don't want to be found, I won't be." She also knew of at least two who would never give up, but Trace's older brother didn't need to know that.

Logan's lips quirked just a tad. "You may be just what Trace needs."

"Excuse me." Trace clapped his hand on Logan's shoulder. "It's getting a little too close to midnight for my girlfriend to be in your arms."

Logan let go of her, raising his hands like a gun had been pointed at him. "I was just leaving."

Trace pulled her against him, nice and close, and her body relaxed into his rhythm.

"What did he want?"

She gazed into Trace's warm brown eyes. "He was worried I would break your heart. Isn't that funny?"

He didn't smile. "That's not—"

The music stopped and the DJ drowned out everything with a ten-second countdown. Trace grinned and counted aloud.

The whole scene reminded her of the days when she and Uncle Joey sat in front of the television and watched the ball drop in New York. She hoped he was seeing it now.

A second after "one" was announced, everyone broke into cheers, except she and Trace. His gaze had softened and he lowered his head to kiss her.

She felt the difference at once. It wasn't a sexual kiss like the others. It was gentle and sweet, like she was precious to him, a feeling she hadn't had since she was five and her parents kissed her goodnight together, yet it was different, a grown-up precious. She liked it.

Trace pulled away and stared at her until Lacey pulled him around and gave him a New Year's kiss on the cheek.

Whisper stood and watched everyone hugging and kissing while *Auld Lang Syne* played loudly from the speakers. As she scanned the room, she noticed the woman, Hailey, staring at her. She shivered. Why did that woman think she knew her? She'd never seen her before.

She lost sight of her when Lacey pulled her into a hug. "Happy New Year."

She returned the greeting until Lacey pulled away.

"Come with me." Lacey hooked her arm and proceeded to the back of the house.

"Where's Cole?"

Lacey glanced back. "I think he's up there by the DJ."

Ah, it was the wedding. "Is your dad making his way back here too?"

Lacey stared at her a moment then laughed, a beautiful, joyous laugh. "Yes, he is. I should have known you would figure it out."

When they reached the east end of the space, Lacey pulled a flower arrangement off the wall. It looked similar to the others hanging in the area, but this one had a handle, long white ribbons and two tiny white doves nestled in it. Lacey moved to another one with shorter ribbons and one dove in it and handed it to her. "Here, you'll need this."

Lacey's dad had Kendra on his arm. Kendra looked expectantly at Lacey. "Okay, I'm here. What do you need to talk to me about?"

Lacey walked to another wall decoration that looked just like Whisper's and handed it to Kendra. "I want you two to be my bridesmaids."

Whisper nodded.

"I'd be happy to." Kendra smiled. "When are you getting—oh." Her smile turned into a smirk.

"We start in about one minute. Where is Adriana?"

Lacey was far too short to see over the crowd, so Whisper sought out the red-dressed woman. "She's coming."

Lacey heaved a sigh. "Oh, good."

Whisper was very impressed with Lacey's planning. She

helped Kendra add a train to Lacey's dress that had been hidden on a chair in the back. When she looked up again, she tried to find Trace but didn't see him.

She was excited. She'd never been in a wedding and though they looked boring, she liked what they symbolized. Luckily, television had given her all she needed to know.

"Ready, Dad?" Lacey looked up at her father, though he wasn't even as tall as Whisper.

Lacey's father smiled down at her, a glowing smile as wide as the Grand Canyon. "Whenever you are, sweet pea."

The phrase whisked Whisper back to her childhood when her father said the same words to her before he took her up in his plane. Her heart contracted again with her loss and she clamped her jaw hard to keep her eyes from watering.

Just then Adriana appeared. "Made it."

The last strains of *Auld Ang Syne* finished and everyone cheered, but when the traditional wedding march began, the room went silent. The partygoers looked around. Kendra took the lead, parting the crowd.

Lacey signaled her to follow and Whisper went in step behind Kendra, the honor Lacey had bestowed on her finally sinking in. A warmth settled in her heart. She'd made a friend. She hadn't had one of those since she was eleven, back before Joey decided they had to move more in order to stay ahead of her relatives.

She caught sight of Trace's aunt. The woman stood open-mouthed. She eventually snapped her mouth shut and turned toward her husband with a scowl. He promptly held up his hand and gave her a furious look. Beverly Hatcher swallowed hard and turned back to watch the progress down the opening in the crowd, her lips pursed together in disapproval.

Whisper had to smile slightly at that. It served the woman

right. She should respect her son's decision in a wife, and Lacey was everything he needed. As she continued to walk by the surprised but smiling faces, she searched for Trace. She was almost to the DJ when she found him standing next to Logan, who stood next to Dillion. She glanced at the groom, who'd she'd met earlier in the evening. He'd said all the right words, thanking her for helping Lacey against the animal abuser, but she sensed a reserve.

Her gaze swung back to Trace. He looked more like a bridegroom than Cole in her opinion. If they were to marry, she'd want him to wear— She caught herself at the thought even as she turned and followed Kendra to the side. Married? Her heart beat erratically as the idea blossomed. She'd never considered she would. She'd never thought beyond taking care of Uncle Joey. Maybe subconsciously she figured she'd be too old to marry after he passed because she expected him to live a very long time.

But what if she found someone like Trace, who understood and cared about Joey? She started to smile when another thought hit her. The money. What would her husband think about the money? He'd probably love it. She scowled. Once again the damn money would rule her life. If it wasn't for Joey's medical bills, she'd give the whole inheritance away to charity. It was nothing but a pain in her ass.

"Whisper?" Kendra leaned toward her. "It's a wedding. There's no need to scowl."

She snapped her head to the side to meet Kendra's gaze. The woman had a smile on her own face. "Sorry. I was thinking of something else." She looked at Lacey's ecstatic face and gave it her full effort. She was happy for Lacey.

She glanced beyond the bride to look at Trace. His gaze was already on her, his look telling her far more than she could understand from so far away. Damn, he was a good-looking cowboy and he had a good heart. She could do worse. What would he think about the money? He didn't have any, so he'd either be thrilled or... What if he wanted to spend it all?

Whisper shook her head to stop her thoughts. She liked the man, but that didn't mean they would get married. Besides, he'd probably get tired of her strangeness and settle down again, this time with some cowgirl who really knew how to ride a horse.

An elbow to her ribs caught her unawares. "Oh."

Kendra whispered, "Stop frowning."

Shit. She put a half smile on her face and watched the bridal couple for the rest of the ceremony. It was the only way to show she was happy for them, which she was. It was her own situation that pissed her off.

Trace couldn't wait for the ceremony to be over. He was happy for Cole and Lacey, but their wedding made him want to whisk Whisper away and make love to her. He didn't even question his need to be her first as an adult. He wanted to explore her body as much as he loved exploring her mind.

Once Lacey and Cole shared their first kiss as a married couple, his palms started to sweat. The bridal couple could stay all night for all he cared.

Maybe there would be cake leftovers because he was leaving…with Whisper. When Whisper had agreed to come to the party as long as she be allowed to leave when she wanted, he'd expected her to want to go long before he was ready. He was ready now.

His brother started to move toward the center of their line and hooked arms with Kendra before following Adriana and Dillion. Trace grinned at Whisper, happy to see her half smile and gray eyes lighting up as he approached. He linked his arm with hers and led her down the impromptu aisle. "Did you like the ceremony?"

She looked at him. "It was boring in parts, but I'm happy for Lacey."

He chuckled, loving her honesty. "Would you be interested in leaving soon, or did you want to stay for the cake and the throwing of the bouquet?"

"I'm ready to leave." She looked at the crowd and frowned.

He glanced in the direction she looked, his protective instincts kicking in, but he didn't see anyone threatening. The only person looking in their direction was the woman named Hailey. Ah, it finally clicked. Whisper didn't want to be recognized.

An unbidden thought rose in his head. He didn't need Whisper's intuitive genius to put the pieces together. She lived in a trailer completely off the grid and said she preferred animals over people. Was she wanted by the law? Shit.

He continued to smile as they brought up the rear of the procession, his emotions spinning like a desert dust devil. Could she have shot someone? She'd certainly shot up Ray Norton. If she did, his gut told him it would be because she protected herself, or someone else, like she had with Lacey. Maybe someone had threatened uncle Joey. He breathed easier at his conclusions.

They finally made it to the end just as Lacey and Cole took the floor for their first dance. He didn't let Whisper disengage from his arm, but continued to walk around the room, grabbing his hat and her cape from the table where they had sat for the dinner. When they reached the door, he stepped aside and let her exit. Settling his hat on his head, he quickly closed the door behind them.

He took a deep breath of the cool night air. If he didn't know better, he'd swear there was a touch of moisture in it.

The door opened behind him. "Whisper Adams."

Trace spun around to find Detective Sean Anderson standing there in a shirt and tie, his sport coat long gone, and a small pad and pen in his hand.

"Is there a problem, Sean?"

"Yes. This woman has eluded us for almost a week. I need to talk to her about the shoot-out in the canyon."

Trace kept his back to Whisper, determined to make the man go through him to get to her. "It's not even one in the morning. Don't you think this could wait until tomorrow? We can come down to the station if you like."

The detective raised a brow at his use of the word "we" but he didn't care.

"That's a nice offer, but I'm determined to take one day off this season. I was here on Christmas and Lacey told me what happened. But right now, it's her word against Ray Norton's and a second witness would help."

"Now is fine." Whisper stepped up next to him. "I'd rather do it here."

He looked at her. "Are you sure?"

She nodded, so he took her hand. "Then let's go over to my truck."

Sean nodded and followed them.

The truck was parked far enough away that they could hear each other. The other advantage in Trace's mind was it wasn't well lit. If Whisper had something to hide, he knew it would show on her face and he was determined to keep Ray Norton in jail and Whisper out of it. He'd heard the whole story from Cole and Lacey, and it could reflect badly on Whisper if viewed differently.

Whisper let go of his hand and faced the detective straight on. He was both proud of her and scared for her at the same time.

Sean started to ask questions and Trace gritted his teeth to keep from interrupting. But when Whisper said Ray Norton was only alive because Lacey wouldn't let her kill him, he had to step in. "I'm sure she would have held back on her own at the last second. She was teaching him a lesson, an eye for an eye. He abused Angel and she let him know what it felt like."

Sean raised his brow at him again, but didn't buy it.

At least she hadn't killed the man and she admitted she wouldn't have because of Lacey, so there was no "intent" to kill, but he could see the fine line she was balanced on.

"I think I have everything I need. Don't leave town in case I need more specifics. Your story corroborates Lacey's exactly, so Norton should go away for a long time, but we may need you on the witness stand."

Sean was too busy putting away his notepad to notice Whisper's tension. She didn't like the idea of testifying, but kept silent. Shit, when had he become so adept at reading her?

Sean held out his hand to Whisper. "Thank you for being honest and talking to me here." The man smiled. "I'm looking forward to a day off tomorrow with my family. Usually this town is quiet and I hope it stays that way."

Trace wrapped his arm around Whisper as they watched the detective go inside. Whisper's preference to talk to Sean out here instead of in the police station sent more smoke signals that not all was as it appeared with her. But he didn't want to think about that tonight, or rather this morning.

When the door closed, Whisper stepped away and reached for the door handle of his truck, but he grabbed her hand. "Hey, where're you going?"

"You said you would take me home." There was anxiousness in her voice.

He pulled her toward him, wanting to reassure her, but

his mind slowed as his body reacted to hers when she came against him. "I thought we could have our second kiss of this year under the moonlight."

He released her hand and she wrapped her arms around his neck. "There is no moonlight tonight."

Glancing at the sky, he chuckled. "I should have known you would have noticed that. How about our second kiss of the year beneath the stars?"

"Okay." Whisper lifted her mouth to his and kissed his lips chastely before pulling back.

"Hey, what was that?"

She tilted her head to the side. "That was the preamble. If you want the full experience, you need to bring me home, now."

He grinned. "Fine, I'll drive you home because I definitely want the whole experience."

She nodded as if they'd settled something important then stepped away. "Come on. I can't wait much longer."

Holy shit. Was she just anxious to get away from the party or was she ready to jump into bed with him? He took his handkerchief from his coat pocket and wiped his brow. The woman could rev up his libido in two seconds. He grabbed the keys out of his jeans pocket and clicked the button that opened the doors.

Whisper climbed in immediately, and he closed the door for her. As he walked around the truck, his mind took over and his concerns about her past floated to the surface again. Jumping in, he forcefully quelled them. There was always tomorrow for that. Tonight was the start of a brand new year, and he planned to start it off in the arms of the woman he lov—

His hand stilled as he reached for the ignition. Shit, he couldn't. He wasn't ready. He just liked her a bunch.

"What's wrong?" Whisper looked at him, the muted light

from the building reflected in her eyes, making them appear silver, like the stars themselves.

Shit. He needed to stop thinking or he'd ruin everything. "Nothing."

"You're lying. What is it?"

He shook his head and started the engine. "Yes, it was something, but not something I'm going to share right now."

She frowned, but sat back and looked out the front window.

"Hey, you're too far away. Scoot over here where Joey sat, so I can be close to you."

She made a show of unbuckling her seatbelt and moving over, belting the middle one over her lap. "Happy now?"

She sounded irritated, but as he started the drive back to her trailer, she relaxed. By the time he'd parked the car, her hand was on his leg, her head rested on his shoulder and his cock was harder than ironwood.

She lifted her head and unbuckled, removing her hand from its teasing position.

Trace reminded himself that he had to take it slow with her. Hell, he might not even be able to push inside her, so he needed to cool down. He jumped out of the truck, but by the time he reached her door, she'd already climbed out.

He walked her to the trailer, hoping for that invitation inside. She opened the door and held it for him. Guess that was his invitation.

He grinned as he took off his hat and stepped inside. No "Would you like a cup of coffee?" or "Would you like to come in for a nightcap?" Nope, Whisper just held the door open.

Inside, she took off her cape and threw it on Joey's bed in the living room. "The bedroom's back here." She walked through a narrow hallway with two doors opposite each other. He assumed one would be the bathroom.

Her bedroom was the complete width of the trailer plus a slide out and it was long. Not cramped at all. It wasn't cheap either. Plush carpet lay beneath his boots and a state-of-the-art television was mounted in the wall opposite the bed. Of course, she had no satellite dish so that was worthless, but it did indicate to him that she was on the grid at some point.

The shelves around the television were jam-packed with books. They were piled on top of each other, taking up every tiny space possible. He looked at the titles to see if he'd recognize any. There was a volume of Shakespeare's complete works, a history of the world, beginner carpentry, *A Christmas Carol*, and a whole set of encyclopedias on animals. Each book focused on a group. He had to ask her if she'd found any useful information on horses. Turning to face her, his question died on his lips.

Chapter Seven

Whisper had taken off her blouse and camisole and was working on the buttons on the side of her skirt. His gaze focused on her breasts as they moved with her actions. When she undid the last button, the skirt fell to the floor and she was naked to her boots.

Holy shit! If he'd known she'd gone commando, he would have left the party before dinner.

She bent over, picked up the skirt and turned to a hidden closet behind the bed. After opening a panel, she pushed a button and he heard the hum of a motor. She hung the skirt on a hanger and closed the panel.

When she turned around his breath caught. She was so much woman. Full breasts were held above a four-pack stomach, wide hips and shapely thighs that cradled a neat bush of black pubic hair. He remembered how soft it felt against his hand.

She sat on the bed and tugged off her boots as if he weren't even in the room. He'd never been with a woman who was so comfortable in her own skin. It was incredibly attractive.

She stood. "Aren't you getting undressed?" She looked at him expectantly.

He'd never had a woman ask him *that*. "Yes."

He dropped his hat on a side table and hung his sport

jacket on a wall hook that was empty. He started to unbutton his shirt, keeping an eye on her.

She reached up and pulled hair pins from her head until her long hair flowed down her back.

Trace stilled. Just when he thought she couldn't be more beautiful, more fascinating, more alive, she moved to another level.

She massaged her head then fluffed out the silky mass. "Now I remember why I don't put my hair up. It's too heavy."

He swallowed. How the hell was he supposed to take it slow when she looked good enough to eat?

"Do you need help?" Her question caught him off guard, but as she walked toward him, it registered.

"I think I do."

He watched her as she focused on the rest of his shirt buttons. Wasn't he supposed to undress her?

She tugged his shirt out from his jeans and finished her task. Then she put her hands under the shirt and pulled it down his arms, her breasts pressing against his bare chest as she worked it all the way to his wrists where the cuffs were still buttoned.

He took a deep breath, loving the feel of her hardening nipples. "You need to unbutton the sleeves."

She didn't say anything, just moved to do what was needed to get his shirt off. Once his wrists were free, she stepped around him and hung it on the hook.

She came back and went for the zipper on his jeans. He caught her hands. "Whoa, wait. I need to take off my boots."

She looked down. "Oh, yeah. Sit."

He did as she commanded, curious as to how she would help when there wasn't much space between the end of the bed and the television wall. It was a nice, big bed.

She turned her back on him and spread her legs. "Lift your leg."

He lifted his new black cowboy boot between her legs and she bent over to pull it off. His pulse raced at the view of her rounded ass and he swallowed hard.

"Lift the other one."

He did as instructed, but couldn't allow her to get away without touching her. With any other woman, her position would have been an invitation to another kind of sex, but this was Whisper, so he simply squeezed her butt. It was soft, womanly and enticing.

She pulled away. "What was that for?"

He grinned. "Just a thank you."

She looked at him as if he was the one who was odd, again reminding him that her sexual experiences had to be limited. Obviously, she hadn't even been touched on her ass. That thought sobered him and gave him the control he needed to keep from jumping her right there.

He stood and before she could touch him, he undid his belt and unzipped his jeans to let his cock breathe. He didn't look at her as he stepped out of his pants and turned to hang them by the belt loop. He'd love it if she pressed herself against his back, but she probably wouldn't know how exciting that could be.

When he turned back, he expected her to still be standing there, but she'd moved to the side of the bed and pulled the covers down. Despite her comfort with her body, he sensed a stiffness in her movements.

He strode around to where she held the cover and took it from her. Lifting her hand, he kissed her palm. Of course, he couldn't let it go at that and he licked her life line.

She pulled her hand away. "That tickles."

"What about this?" He took her other hand and brought her index finger into his mouth and sucked.

When he released her finger, he looked at her. "Well?"

"I like that."

The memory of their time by the shed flitted through his mind and he brought his hands up to cup her breasts. She liked her breasts played with the most, probably because she didn't know any other touch could be as stimulating.

He watched her expression as he brought his thumbs up to stroke back and forth across her hard nipples. What he wanted to do was bring her body flush with his, but the second his cock touched her, she might go into "acceptance" mode and when he penetrated her, if he could, he wanted her to crave it as much as he did.

She watched his fingers even as her breathing accelerated, but she made no move to touch him.

He lowered his head and heard the smallest intake of breath from her. Cupping one breast while his hand played with the other, he flicked the nipple with his tongue.

"More." Whisper's demand fueled his hunger for her and he pulled the nipple and areola into his mouth. While he sucked, he flicked the hard nub.

"Trace." Her breathy word sent sparks racing through his veins.

His name on her lips was like a match thrown onto a scrub brush during a drought. To know she enjoyed his touch started a fire low in his belly. He switched to the other nipple and sucked that one as well, but when he released it, he nibbled it with his teeth.

Her hands grasped his shoulders, revealing her pleasure.

He continued his attention to her nipple, tugging at it with his teeth and circling it with his tongue. Her hands dug into his shoulders, making it clear she was ready to lie down.

Lifting his head, he met her dark, stormy gray gaze. Desire was written all over her face from her eyes to her open mouth, where tiny quick breaths escaped. He couldn't resist her lips and pulled her upper body close.

An inch from the kiss, he whispered, "I want the full experience this time."

Her lips met his and she opened for him, letting him sweep inside her mouth like his cock wanted to plunge inside her sheath. Tasting champagne mixed with the minty flavor of Whisper, he stroked her tongue. Hers met his and he allowed her to explore his mouth. She moaned deep in her throat as he caught her tongue and sucked. It wasn't a shy moan, as if she tried to hide how much he pleased her. It was a deep-throated, husky moan that sent need straight to his cock.

Her pelvis pressed against him, but his mind signaled him to go slow, even though her mons pushed against his cock, the soft hair tantalizing him. He'd lose control if she continued that. Reluctantly, he ended the kiss, easing out of it with nibbles on her lips and chaste kisses to the corners of her mouth, wanting to show her exactly how important she was to him.

Her dazed look cleared and she gave him a half smile, the one that sent his heart into overdrive. "You're a good kisser."

He grinned, despite knowing she didn't have much to compare him to. Hell, it still felt good.

"Can we get on the bed now?"

His grin widened. "Of course."

He loosened his hold and she dropped onto the bed. "Good, my knees weren't going to hold me much longer."

He chuckled. He'd had no idea how rewarding it could be to make love with such unadulterated honesty. Thank God he had no doubts about his prowess in bed. His wife may have wanted his money more than him, but she never complained about their bedroom activities.

Shit, why did he have to think about her now? His body cooled instantly.

"Why are you frowning?" Whisper lay on her back, her hip-length hair thrown to one side and her curvy body just waiting to be pleasured.

He lowered his brows more. "There so much I want to do to you to make you enjoy this, I'm having a hard time deciding what to do first."

She shrugged. "That's easy. Suck on my nipples."

His cock returned to its hard state quickly. "Thank you, that helps." It took a lot of effort to avoid smiling.

"And then when I'm wetter, you can slide your finger inside me like you did yesterday."

He fisted his hands at her words and his cock jumped, something he couldn't control.

She noticed. "Is something wrong?"

He took a calming breath. "No." At her look of disbelief, it was apparent he'd have to be as honest as she was. "Your words get me excited, which makes it harder to hold back until I can give you an orgasm."

"But I'm already wet."

Count to ten. One. Two. Three. Four... By time he reached ten, he had some semblance of control. Luckily, she didn't say anything else and just stared at his chest.

As much as he wanted to crawl between her legs immediately, his concern over her automatic response toward acceptance instead of enjoyment helped him to walk to the other side of the bed and lie down next to her. He propped himself up on his side so he could view her. "Your body is beautiful."

She looked at him but didn't say anything. He loved that she didn't deny his words. "Do you like the way I look?"

She nodded. "Especially your chest...a lot."

"So touch it."

She glanced warily at him before hesitantly placing her hand on him. "I like that you're warm." Her hand moved to his abdominal muscles. "And hard."

He wanted her to move that hand down farther, but she reversed her direction and brushed over his right pectoral.

"Your nipple is hard like mine get."

Shit, that boy who introduced her to sex had left out a lot. "Yes, and they feel to me like yours feel to you."

"Really?" She looked unconvinced. "So if I suck on them, they will get harder and you'll feel that pressure between your legs?"

His cock jumped again. Shit, this would be the toughest lovemaking he'd ever done, no doubt about it. "Yup." He tried to be nonchalant about it, but the idea that she might make her own move had his stomach tensing with anticipation.

Luckily, her attention was on his chest so she didn't see his cock's reaction to her words. He'd noticed she avoided looking below his waist, more confirmation she had no idea what pleasure his erection could give her.

She turned on her side to face him. He held his breath as she stared at his pectoral. *Yes, do it.*

No sooner did he have the thought then she leaned forward and took his nipple into her mouth, copying what he'd done to her exactly.

Fire-like pleasure shot straight to his cock, and he held himself back from grabbing her by the barest control.

She let go and inspected his nipple. "I like that."

He grimaced. "So do I." Luckily, her gaze was fixed on his very hard nub.

"Do you like this?" She reached toward his other nipple, her intent clear.

Quickly, he rolled her over onto her back. "I like it too much."

She gave him her smirk.

He shook his head. "I need more of you first. That's all."

Whisper glanced downward but she couldn't see his throbbing cock pressed into the sheets. "You want to—"

"No, I want to give you pleasure and hopefully an orgasm."

She lowered her brows. "But I told you I'm already wet. You can check."

He couldn't smile to reassure her because his cock was determined to see exactly how wet she was. Wet? Orgasm? Hell, she thought being wet meant she had an orgasm. "Whisper. Exactly how old were you the last time you had sex?"

"Sixteen."

She said she was thirty. Damn, he hadn't realized how close to the truth he'd been. She was practically a virgin. Unless she'd watched porn, which he highly doubted. She probably thought she knew everything from watching animals mate.

"You're frowning again. If you don't want to have sex, that's okay."

He closed his eyes. The emotions running through him too mixed up to let her see. Excitement, nervousness, need, caring— all caused his gut to tense. He wanted to make this special for her.

He opened his eyes and stared into her gray gaze, so puzzled by his actions. "I want to make love to you very much." He felt her tension ease. "I'm struggling with how much I want to make love to you and how much I want you to enjoy it."

"Oh, I will."

He shook his head. "No, not like you did when you were a teenager. You are an adult now, with an adult body and an adult man here to show you how much enjoyment you really can get from this experience."

She looked doubtful. "Are you saying there is more to it than what I've had and that I will like this other part?"

He loved that she was so quick. "Exactly."

She looked away as she contemplated that for a moment. Finally, her gaze returned to his. "I always wondered what all the excitement was about. You're saying I can feel like you feel when you come?"

He nodded.

Whisper's eyes grew dark. "Please. Show me."

His heart melted and a new confidence filled him. "You said you were wet. That is your body preparing for my cock to enter your opening."

She nodded, her eyes alight with interest.

"That's just the beginning. An orgasm will take over your whole body in exquisite pleasure. It is impossible to put into words and the only way to understand it is to have one."

"And you need to be inside me so I can have one?"

He shook his head. "No, I want to give you your first orgasm without having one of my own. Then we can do it together. How's that sound?"

Her lips twitched up at the corners just a bit. "It sounds interesting. What do I do?"

He grinned. "Just lie there and relax."

"I can do that." She gave him her half smile, her excitement at learning more communicating itself to his body.

She would definitely have the easy part of this if he did it right. He wished he had an ice cube right now to rub along his cock. The damn thing was far too excited. Then a thought occurred. "Stay right here."

He rose from the bed and rifled through his sport jacket. His fingers grasped the condoms he put in there and he brought them back to the bed.

"What are you doing?"

He threw the condoms on the sheet to be within easy reach. "I'm getting us protection."

"Oh, I totally forgot. I'm not ready to be a mother yet."

He stilled as a vision of Whisper showing her daughter how to shoot flitted across his mind. It was far too distracting to hold on to, and he let it go as he resumed his spot next to her, his cock behaving a bit better while he focused on his responsibility.

Whisper lay on her back, watching his every move. He leaned forward and gave her a gentle kiss, keeping his erection from touching her. When he finished letting her know exactly how much she meant to him, he ran his fingers through the mound of black hair at the juncture of her legs.

"I'd like to feel your wetness. Can you spread your legs for me?"

She did, immediately.

He smiled inside at her eagerness to learn. Careful to keep his hips from her body, so she wouldn't switch gears, he spread her folds with his fingers. Her juices coated her opening and his cock hardened more. "Did you like my finger inside you last time we were together?"

"Yes. It feels good when you suck my nipples."

His balls tightened at her words. Shit, she was so blunt, making this "lesson" extra hard for him. He leaned over and nipped at her nipple before sucking it in while he slid his finger inside her moist sheath.

"Yes, I like that." She lifted her hips toward his hand.

He slowly moved his finger in and out while he paid attention to her breasts.

She moaned, her hips pressing upward against his hand.

After releasing her nipple, he leaned back, his finger still buried inside her.

She opened her eyes. "I liked that."

He smiled seductively and her eyes widened. There was so much he wanted to teach her, but this first time he needed to keep it simple.

This time when he slid his finger out of her opening, he coated her clit with her wetness.

"Oh! What was that?"

"That's your clit. It's going to bring you to orgasm."

She didn't respond. Instead, she closed her eyes.

He sank his finger back inside her and rubbed his thumb across her clit.

Her breathing grew more rapid as he swirled her nub, watching her reactions with a keen eye. He wanted to build it slowly for her.

He increased the speed and pressure of his thumb, back and forth over her hard clit. Her sheath squeezed his finger in response.

"What…" A groan followed her question. "Oh, yes." The wonder in her voice helped him keep his control.

She deserved this and he would make it perfect for her. The honor of bringing her to her first orgasm helped him keep his focus. He increased the speed of his movement more, rubbing her clit, keeping the pressure where it should feel the best. Her moans became continuous.

Carefully, he pulled his index finger from her and added another finger, sliding both inside her pussy. Her sheath stretched to accommodate them this time.

Whisper's breaths came faster and her pelvis tilted to keep her clit in contact with his thumb. God, he wanted to kiss her right now, but he had to be happy with watching her have her first orgasm, a vision he ached to see.

Her voice grew louder, her hips more insistent as she instinctually pushed to the pressure she craved. She was so close.

He lowered his head and pulled her rosy nipple into his mouth, sucking.

"Ahhh!" Whisper's yell as she hit her climax rocked his heart. Her legs crossed as she pushed her clit against his thumb, her hips rising from the bed as her body vibrated with pleasure.

He kept the pressure on her nub, releasing her nipple to watch her. Her stomach rose and fell with her breaths and he could see the rhythm of her heart ripple her belly. Her lips were slightly parted, her cheeks flushed and her head turned slightly to the side.

He waited in anticipation of seeing her eyes.

When her legs relaxed, he withdrew his fingers and pressed his whole body against her side, unable to resist the draw of her any longer.

He'd never had the opportunity to bring a woman her first orgasm. This was important…for both of them.

Whisper finally opened her eyes and stared at the ceiling a moment, then turned her head and looked at him. Her gaze was almost black, but even as she focused on him it slowly turned to the gray he loved. "That was an orgasm?"

He nodded, unable to keep the smile from his face.

She returned his smile, not with her signature smirk or half smile, but with a full face, eyes crinkling, blow-him-away smile.

His life seemed to finally fall into focus in that one beautiful vision. He pulled her head toward him and gave her a gentle kiss.

Her hand locked on to his neck and she pulled her body flush against him even as her tongue breached his lips, but neither of them deepened the kiss. It was a kiss of completion, satisfaction and connection.

She pressed her pelvis against his cock and wrapped her leg over his, a good sign she might be ready for him. He held her tight, loving the feel of her along his length. They were almost the same height and every curve of hers melded into him.

She pulled her head back and gazed into his eyes. "That was…indescribable."

He grinned. "That's good." He ran his hand down her back and through her silky hair. She smelled good, felt good, and tasted good.

She looked away for a moment and then returned her gaze to him. "Thank you. I didn't know. I feel like… It's as if you gave me a new life."

His heart lurched at her comment and he gathered her tight against him. He wanted to know so much about her, teach her about making love, riding horses and—His hand stilled even as his heart swelled. He wanted to love her.

He stroked her back again, well aware of how quick she was to pick up on a person's vibes.

She pulled her head from his shoulder. "So do you want to go in me now?"

He shook his head. "Not quite yet."

Her brow furrowed. "But I thought that was the point of sex."

"Not exactly. Well, yes, that is what it is with animals, but us humans make everything complicated, including sex."

She pulled back some more. "I don't think so. You know, I've had sex before even if I didn't have an orgasm."

"I stand corrected." He used his finger to trace a lazy circle over her areola. "Sex is like you expect, but making love means pleasure like you just experienced, only together."

Whisper swallowed. "Love?"

"You've heard that term, right? Making love?"

She'd thought she was in love with her first boyfriend but

over the years she realized it was just infatuation. Did Trace love her? He'd just given her the best experience of her life. She was grateful. She cared about him, but love?

"Whisper?"

She snapped her gaze back to him. "Yes."

"So you have heard the term 'making love'?"

"Of course." It was a term, that's all. She heard it used in movies and on television shows. "I just thought it meant sex. It does, doesn't it?"

"Yes, but it's more than that. It's sex with a connection." He looked away. "It means something. Sex is just sex."

She didn't say anything. Trace seemed to be working out something for himself. She couldn't imagine having sex just for sex. Even her old boyfriend was someone she liked when they weren't having sex. Maybe Trace wondered if his wife used him for that too.

Whisper's heart hurt at that thought. He was a good man. What his wife did was wrong. She should go to jail, not make off with his money.

It was just like her own relatives, trying to snatch her to be her guardian and then later wanting to drug her to sign everything over. The last attempts were to commit her because she was "psychologically unstable." They told others it was for her own good, but they didn't make it a secret from her that they wanted her inheritance.

She understood how Trace must feel and she pressed her hand to his cheek. "Do you still want to make love?"

His gaze returned to her, and she sucked in her breath. His copper eyes looked at her as if he needed her just to breathe. She didn't know why, but she wrapped her hand around his neck and brought his lips to hers. She gave him the kind of kiss he'd given her at midnight, happy he'd come into her life.

When she pulled away, he stared at her a moment before his lips quirked upward in a crooked smile. "I like that, and you just gave me an idea."

She watched him, waiting to see what his next idea was. She definitely liked his ideas, but when he pulled away from her and lay on his back, she wasn't so sure anymore.

"I'm all yours. You can make love to me. Do what you want, what makes *you* feel good."

A thrill raced up her back and her vagina tightened. "And I can tell you what I want?"

He nodded.

She smirked and straddled him across his waist. "I think I'm going to like this." She leaned over and lowered her breast to his mouth.

He didn't hesitate. He licked around her areola and flicked at her hardening nipple. Then, as if he anticipated her wish, he took the hard nub in his teeth and pulled. Need shot from her breast to her pussy and her thighs contracted against him. She started to lift herself up to give him her other breast, but he held on to her nipple, flooding her with a strange sensation that had her juices flowing.

He clamped his mouth onto that breast and sucked gently. "More."

He increased the suction and her folds filled with her juices. She arched her back, pushing her breast toward him while pressing her pelvis against him.

Her thighs moved back and the hair above his cock brushed against her clit. The spike of exhilaration that went through her body came out her mouth. "Ow."

Trace immediately released her nipple. "Did I hurt you?"

"No. I…I brushed against your hair." She sat up on him, scooting back more. She felt his cock laying between her legs, but it didn't bother her. It was all in her hands when she'd take him inside.

She pointed to his hair. "That rubbed against my clit and it felt good."

"Let me see." Before she knew what he was about, he'd used his fingers to separate her folds and then brushed them across her clit.

The movement sang through her sheath and it contracted with wanting. As he continued to play with her, she found her hips moving forward and back as she glided over his cock. "That feels good."

He continued his play with one hand and his other came up to tweak her nipples, back and forth from one to the other, even as his fingers went back and forth across her clit.

Her need built for that orgasm she knew was possible, but it was just beyond her reach. She arched her back, presenting him with her breasts, hoping the pinches and twirls would get her there, but they didn't. She pulled her whole body back in frustration. "It's not happening."

Trace lowered his hands to his hard stomach. "Why not?"

"I need your fingers inside me."

He shook his head. "What you need inside you is my cock."

She looked at his hard erection now sticking up in front of her. A penis had never brought her to fulfillment before, but she trusted him to show her that nirvana again. The memory of her first orgasm had her willing to try anything.

Lifting herself up, she positioned herself over him. "You're sure?"

"Yes, but come down slowly. You're very tight."

"And you're very big." But there was only one way to see if he would fit.

Chapter Eight

Slowly, Whisper lowered herself until his head touched her opening. Still doubtful, she let herself move down an inch.

Her sheath stretched at the intrusion, but it didn't hurt, so she went a little farther. "Oh, it feels full." As she lowered herself a little more, she felt that same flood of sensation that she had when he didn't release her nipple. It was a strange mix of helplessness and anticipation, and her juices flowed, making the last few inches an easy glide.

She sat still, fully impaled by Trace's cock and took stock of every feeling coursing through her. Her nipples were harder and ached, her clit pulsed as if waiting and her stomach was rolling around like a coyote scratching his back in the desert.

"How's it feel?" Trace's face looked tense, though his voice was calm.

"Different. Exciting."

He let out a breath. "Good, because you need to do it again."

"What?"

He threw his arm out and grabbed a condom. "You don't want to get pregnant, right?"

"No." She pulled herself off him fast and was immediately unhappy with the loss of the added pressure within her.

"Ugh." Trace closed his eyes as if he were in pain.

Shit, what did she do? Tired of showing how ignorant she was, she waited.

Finally, he opened his eyes. "Warn me next time you're going to get off. I almost came and that would have spoiled it for you."

"Already?" Even her old boyfriend didn't come that fast, though not much longer.

"Whisper, you haven't had sex in fourteen years, which is why your sheath is so tight. It's also why it feels so good and makes it hard for me to stay in control. After we have made love a number of times, it should loosen a bit, which will greatly help me."

A number of times? He wanted to do this again? Her heart warmed at the prospect. She liked how he made her feel.

In no time, Trace had the condom on and she was straddled over him again. This time she knew what to expect, but it was still tight, especially with the extra layer. When she had completely impaled herself again, she sighed. It *did* feel good.

Trace grasped her waist. "Don't move."

She hadn't planned on moving. She wasn't even sure how to, but sitting with him inside her was good enough for her.

After a minute, Trace's hands moved up her torso to cup her breasts. Just like he had before, he stroked his thumbs across her nipples. This time when the thrill from his touch went down between her legs, it was intensified, moving around her sheath and the cock inside. Her juices flowed at this new feeling.

He changed his movement and took both nipples between his thumb and fingers and pinched lightly. The feelings that coursed from her breasts to her pussy zinged through her, making her hips move involuntarily as she arched into his touch.

Her clit brushed against his pelvis, adding another layer of excitement streaming throughout her body. "Oh. I love that."

Trace continued to play with her nipples, alternately pinching and twirling, and the ache between her legs grew even as she rocked against him, her clit sending more pleasure to her core. It was too much.

She tried to pull back her chest but Trace latched on. Heat spread through her at the helpless feeling that swept her up, forcing her to rub her clit against him. She grasped his arms, unable to stop pushing against him.

Her orgasm was coming. It was just around the corner. She could feel it.

Trace's hands left her nipples and grabbed her waist, holding her against him as his pelvis pushed upward. "Whisper!"

Her orgasm exploded through her. Every nerve ending came alive as the cascade of ecstasy lifted her beyond herself, yet kept her hips grinding against the warmth filling her as Trace came. She was alive, free, filled with joy.

Finally, she wrangled control of her body and slowed her movements, still feeling spurts of sensation until her breathing calmed and she was able to stop reaching for every last spark of thrill.

She opened her eyes to find Trace watching her. She smiled. How could she not? He gave her so much and was so kind. That orgasm was even better than the last.

He grinned, completely proud of himself. "So what do you think?"

"I think that was awesome." She ran her hand over his chest, loving the way his hard stomach muscles contracted as she went. "I also think that I need to read more about sex. Uncle Joey's birds-and-bees talk was lacking a few details."

Trace chuckled, his body moving under her, causing sweet aftershocks to ping between her legs.

"That's usually a talk the mom gives. I don't imagine Uncle Joey knew exactly what to say to you."

She sobered, the mention of the word "mom" bringing the usual ache to her heart. She started to lift and halted. "I'm getting off now. Are you ready?"

"Wait." He moved his hand between her legs, making her think of having sex all over again. "Okay, you can rise now, but do it slowly, please."

She did as he requested and was glad she hadn't rushed it. It was an adjustment not having him inside her. When she crawled off and sat beside him, she saw that he had held the condom on so she wouldn't take it with her.

Trace got up and walked into the bathroom.

She took the opportunity to slide under the blanket and sheet, her body oddly cold without him nearby. She flicked the switch that turned off the main lights and left the low-level floor lighting on, so Trace could find his way back.

He returned in a few minutes and got in beside her. "Come here." He held his arm up.

Guessing he wanted her to lie next to him, she scooted over and put her head on his shoulder. She liked his warmth and threw her leg over his and her arm around his waist. "Hmm, I like this. Is this another part of making love?"

He chuckled, a sound she really enjoyed. "Yes, it is."

The position was comforting, like someone cared about her. She sensed Trace did, which made the feeling even better.

"I want you to tell me about your childhood."

She lifted her head to look at him. "Why?"

"Because I want to know."

She lay her head back down. "Okay, what do you want to know?"

His arm wrapped around her, holding her close against him, completing that feeling of being cared for.

"Tell me how your parents died and how you ended up with Joey."

She was glad she was crushed up against him because she hadn't talked about any of that…ever. She hadn't had to. Joey was there and no one else cared. She hesitated at that. Trace cared.

"My father was a mechanical engineer and he owned his own plane. He used to take me up in it for rides. We lived in Tucson then. Mom and Dad decided to go to Flagstaff for the weekend. I was to stay home with Joey. He is my father's brother. My parents' plane crashed between Phoenix and Prescott. They were both killed on impact."

Trace's arm squeezed her tight as she paused to swallow the lump in her throat. Talking about it was tough. "That's it."

"So you went to live with Uncle Joey?"

She nodded. Though there had been a three-year custody battle between her uncle and her mother's sister, her parents' will had held. She was always thankful for that. She loved her uncle.

She doubted she would have made it past ten growing up with her cousins Keith and Timmy. Their mother had run through her parents' inheritance in a few years, while her own parents had kept the money safe and growing. She found out later from Joey that her dad had insisted on working and providing for them, despite her mom's wealth.

Trace rubbed her arm, a comforting movement that she appreciated. Even thinking about her parents made her yearn for them, so she rarely did, never mind talk about them.

"You told Hailey you were homeschooled. Was that Joey?"

"Yes. He got me tutors in the subjects he didn't feel

qualified to teach. He was an accountant so he taught me math and science and anything analytical."

"What about friends and doing kid stuff?"

She shrugged. "Some of the places we lived I had some kids my age I played with after they came home from school, but by the time I reached high school age, I didn't have much in common with most teenagers. No loss as far as I could see. That part of human development is strange."

It was more than strange, and by that time, she and Uncle Joey were moving every year and she found her peers boring. Everything was traumatic to them. Luckily, living in trailer parks had exposed her to so much Arizona wildlife and desert that she didn't miss having friends. Besides, now she had Lacey.

"I like Lacey but Cole seems reserved. Do you two get along?" She looked up at him.

His eyes widened. "That was quite the change in subject."

"Do you?"

"Yes, we get along fine…most of the time. Cole is a very by-the-book person, always focused on what's right. He just needs Lacey to straighten him out on what that is once in a while." He grinned.

"And what about you? What do you plan to do when your divorce is final? Do you plan to find another cowgirl to settle down with and build up another ranch?" Her stomach flipped over as she said aloud what she'd been thinking and held her breath, not even sure why it mattered.

Trace's bark of laughter was not what she expected.

"First of all, I didn't marry a cowgirl the first time. I probably should have. And second of all, I haven't even begun to think about life after the divorce. It's hard when I don't know if she's going to get everything including my truck, or if the courts will see the light and give me at least half. That's the way it's *supposed* to be here in this state. Any martial property, which is all we had, is supposed to be split half and half."

He paused and she felt the anger churning inside him.

"I can't make plans until I know what I have and don't have. Besides, I'm perfectly happy at Last Chance, helping the horses who need it and pitching in so Cole and Lacey can have a good homestead. I'd lost touch with the beauty and satisfaction of working on the land instead of overseeing others. Believe it or not, I'm pretty good at mending fences, training horses, and roping cattle. I'm just a bit rusty."

So he was a cowboy after all. "Why are you rusty?"

"I guess you could say my focus changed to being a rancher. There's a difference."

She didn't know that and she stored the information away. But while they were questioning each other, she had something else she wanted to know. "How come you know how to bring a wheelchair upstairs?"

His face softened. "My dad. He had two strokes six months apart. He wasn't as lucky as Joey after the second. Logan and Mom were still at the ranch and cared for him, but I came over at least twice a week to give them a break and to spend time with my dad. He was more verbal than Joey, but physically, he was pretty bad off."

She sensed the grief of his loss, but he seemed to have come to terms with it. A lot better than she had when she lost her parents. "How long ago did he die?"

Trace's lips quirked up at one corner. "Most people say passed away, but it really is the same thing. It was about two years. Logan took it the hardest. He and my dad were very close. I guess you could say I was a mama's boy."

A noise outside the window caught her attention.

It caught Trace's too. He whispered, "Did you hear that?"

She nodded, her body tense. She never knew when Keith and Timmy would find her and noises outside were not a good sign. Luckily, it was usually an animal. She listened carefully.

Trace kept his voice low. "It sounds like someone is trying to get in your shed."

It did sound like that.

"Stay here." Trace rose from the bed and moved to his sport coat. He took what looked like a forty-four magnum from an inside pocket and stood next to the window where he opened the slats in the blinds. After a few minutes he let them drop. "I can't tell. It's too dark outside to see anything."

Whisper rose and walked by him into the kitchen.

"Wait, Whisper."

She threw on her coat and grabbed up Sal. If it was one of her cousins, she didn't want Trace to get hurt.

He grabbed her arm as she reached for the door. "Stop. You need to stay inside."

"Why?"

"Because I need to protect you."

Huh, since when? "I need to protect you."

Trace shook his head, but stopped when a loud noise came from the shed. He looked at her.

"It sounds like scraping." She listened some more but the noise stopped.

Trace held his finger in front of his mouth as he moved to the door. He had his hand on the knob when a loud bray broke the silence.

Whisper laughed with relief. "Damn burrow. Almost gave me a heart attack."

Trace stood rooted to the floor staring at her.

"What?"

He blinked. "I've never heard you laugh."

Really? She laughed a lot. Well, maybe more around Joey. Guess she was feeling more comfortable being around him. She liked that. "I'm sure I'll do it again." She winked. "Now move aside. I need to see what Motley wants."

"Motley?"

She brushed by him, grabbing her flashlight on the way out and strode to the shed. Motley stood there, staring at the building. "What is it now? Are you hurt?"

The burro pawed at the shed.

"Well shit, Motley, I didn't know you were going to be back. I don't have any more hay." She quickly went over in her mind what she had in the trailer. There had to be something he could eat. "Tell you what. I'll get you some water and see what I can find."

Turning to head back to the trailer, she found Trace right behind her in all his naked glory. And it *was* glorious. "Shit, you're going to get stung by a scorpion walking around barefoot."

He looked at her feet. "And you're not?"

"Yeah, I know. I just have to get him some water and find him something to eat." She walked by Trace and headed inside for her old boots. After slipping them on, she came back outside and grabbed a bucket from under the trailer and filled it with water from the outside spigot.

As she lugged it toward the burro, she noticed Trace smoothing his hand over the animal's side. "Careful. He's wild."

Trace looked up. "*He's* also pregnant."

She dropped the bucket down and stared. "Well strip me naked and throw me in a lava pit. I never even checked. Why would I?"

He grinned, his white-toothed smile visible even in the starlight. He should do one of those toothpaste commercials.

"She must need some food."

Trace shook his head. "Not necessarily. My guess is she is going to foal soon and considers this a safe spot."

Whisper liked that. Just the thought of having a baby burro around was enough to make her happy. Happy? She was downright excited. "If she's pregnant then she probably does need food. But there's a palo verde right there, so why scrape at the shed door?"

Trace left the burro and moved toward her. "My guess is you already figured it out. Look at her drink."

They stood side by side watching the burro get her fill of water. Trace put his arm around her and pulled her against his side. "This has to be the best New Year's I've ever had."

She silently agreed.

~~*~~

Trace glanced over at Whisper sitting right next to him. She met his gaze for a moment and gave him a smirk. He returned his attention to the road. He was happy this morning as they drove back to Last Chance Ranch to get Joey.

After the burro incident, he and Whisper had made love again, but despite his intention to do so all night, they fell asleep in each other's arms. For the first time since he'd been served divorce papers, he was honestly happy. What was better, was he saw no reason for why he'd stop being happy for a long time to come.

He drove up to the house and parked his truck. The only vehicles in the yard were Logan's, his grandparents and Lacey's. Cole and Lacey had stayed in a casita at Poker Flat for a weekend honeymoon until Cole could get off work for a week.

Getting out, he didn't make it to the other side in time. "Whisper, you're supposed to allow me to open your door."

She brushed him off. "Really? That's fine when I'm in a skirt, but I'm perfectly able to get out of a truck on my own."

"Plus you're very excited to see Joey, aren't you?"

"Yeah, I —"

A ruckus in the barn interrupted Whisper and they both looked at each other. A loud neigh was followed by more banging. It sounded like a horse was breaking apart the barn.

He turned and ran, Whisper right behind him.

Logan stood across from a stall where a beautiful black horse reared then came down, pounding at the stall door.

"What's going on!" He had to shout over the noise.

Logan ran to them. "Stay away, that horse is mad."

"Where'd he come from?" Trace could see even from the doorway that the horse was showing the whites of his eyes.

"He's another rescue. They dropped him off, all drugged up. We barely got him into the stall because he was so drugged and didn't want to go. I went out with the guy to sign the paperwork and as soon as he left I heard this banging. I don't know what the story is on this one, but he's going to hurt himself if we don't calm him down. Can you stay here while I get far enough away to make a call to Jenna? This boy needs more sedation."

Trace nodded and watched his brother stride away. When he turned around, Whisper stood opposite the stall and his heart lurched up into his throat. "Whisper!"

She ignored him, instead moving closer to the wild horse.

He started for her when she opened the stall door and the horse charged out. He slammed himself up against the wall as it ran by. "Fuck, Whisper, you can't just let out a wild horse." He grabbed her by the arms. "Are you okay?"

She shrugged him off. "Of course I am." She headed for the barn door and he grabbed her arm again. "Wait. You could have been killed. What were you thinking?"

She finally took her focus from the horse and onto him. When she did, her attitude softened, at least as much as Whisper could soften. "You were afraid for me. I didn't mean to scare you. The horse needed to get out."

"What the hell? " Logan's voice outside had Trace fearing for his brother's life now and he ran to the barn door.

The horse stood still next to one of the training corrals, its breathing heavy, its nostrils still flaring, its body shaking, but its ears were back up and it eyes no longer rolling back in its head. Logan stood frozen halfway to the house.

Whisper walked by and approached the horse. She called to Logan. "What's his name?"

Logan looked at her like she was crazy. "Black Jack."

Trace followed her. "Whisper, not every animal will respond to people. Be careful."

She remained focused on the horse as she approached his head. "Black Jack. You're okay now. It's all right." She held out her hand as if she were going to shake hands with the horse then turned her palm toward the ground.

Trace stayed right behind her, ready to push her out of harm's way at the least sign from the horse.

Whisper lowered her arm.

The horse responded by lowering its head.

Trace had never seen anything like that. Still, as Whisper stepped closer, he stayed vigilant.

"Black Jack. You're okay now. No one will put you away again. I promise." She stepped even closer and raised her hand to pet his nose. Black Jack's ears were forward, listening to Whisper, but when she touched him, he nudged her shoulder.

"Good boy. You're okay now." She moved to his side and stroked his neck.

Trace watched in fascination as the horse's breathing evened out and he stopped shaking.

Logan came up behind him. "I wouldn't have believed it if

I hadn't seen it with my own eyes, but I gotta tell you, I'm glad she was able to calm him down. He's a real beauty. I'd hate to see him hurt himself."

Trace had to agree. The black quarter horse had a long mane and tail and a perfect white star on its forehead. "Did you get a hold of Dr. Jenna?"

Logan shook his head. "No. She's at another ranch treating a sick cow, but her office said they'd get word to her."

Trace never stopped watching Whisper and Black Jack, ready to step in if he had to. "Whisper, is he okay?"

She looked at him. "He is now. You can pet him."

Logan stepped past him before he could move. "What was wrong with him and why is he better now?"

She looked Logan in the eyes sternly. "He was panicked. He's claustrophobic. You can never put him in the barn again."

Logan's eyes widened. "It's not too cold here in the winter, but he'll need shelter from the rain. I can't just leave him out here."

She shrugged. "Try a carport then. He can't go in a stall. This isn't just a small issue. This horse is terrified of being closed in."

Logan crossed his arms over his chest. "And you know this how?"

"I just do."

The two glowered at each other, not looking away, and Trace finally stepped between them. He faced Logan. "What's Black Jack's story?"

"I don't know. I didn't even have a chance to look at the paperwork before he started banging down the stall door."

"Maybe we should find out." Trace raised his brows at his brother.

"Fine." Logan went up to the porch and opened a folder on the table there.

Trace turned around to find Whisper watching him.

"I'm right."

He grinned. "I know you are."

Her stance relaxed. "Thank you for that. Most people just think me crazy. Black Jack just doesn't like closed-in spaces."

Trace gave the horse a stroke along its withers before remembering it wouldn't mind being touched on its face. Lightyear had him well-trained.

Logan came back and stared at Whisper before addressing Trace. "She's scary."

"No, she isn't." He frowned at his brother. "She's gifted."

Logan looked at Whisper. "Black Jack was discovered in an old copper mine. Some teenagers heard the horse making a racket and not knowing it was a horse, called in rescue crews."

"It says that the owner had been in the mine with the horse when it started to cave in. He ran out but the horse didn't make it, so he thought Black Jack had been buried alive. When the horse was returned to him days later and he tried to put him back in his old stall, the horse went wild, so animal welfare brought him here on drugs. They think the horse was in that mine for three days."

Trace thought the light made Whisper's eyes look silver, but as she turned toward the horse, he could see the water in her eyes. He hadn't seen her cry before and it bothered him. She was so in tune with animals, it was as if anything they experienced had happened to her.

She stroked the horse along his nose. "You poor boy. You're safe now, Black Jack. They will take good care of you here." She faced Logan with a stern look, all trace of tears gone. "Right?"

His brother stepped up to the horse and gave it a stroke along its neck. "I will personally insure he is well taken care of." The horse nudged Logan's shoulder. Logan switched his gaze to the horse. "Okay, Black Jack. Let's see if the corral is more to your liking." Logan picked up the halter he'd left on the corral fence and methodically put it on.

Whisper stepped away and let him work. Trace couldn't resist her another moment. He was damn proud of her and yet pissed that she'd put herself in danger. Wrapping his arms about her waist from behind, he rested his chin on her shoulder. "I don't think you could ever stop surprising me."

She relaxed against him. "That's only because I'm different." She turned around in his embrace and looped her arms around his neck. "I'm so glad Cole has this place and that you help him. I wish every unwanted and abused horse could come live here."

"I'm afraid that would put Cole in the poor house too quickly and then all the horses here would lose their home. It's better that he finds loving homes for them after they are rehabilitated."

She raised her brow. "You mean like Lightyear?"

He grinned. "Okay, so I've grown a bit attached to him. I may have to buy him from Cole so I can keep him."

"I think that's a great idea. Now can we go get Joey? I'm sure all the activity has made him tired."

Trace didn't want to let her go, but she was right. It was almost noon on New Year's Day and Joey had been in a much busier and louder environment than he was used to. "You're right." He released her, but wasn't happy about it.

They'd made it to the porch when a car pulled into the yard. Trace turned around and groaned. "Now what is *she* doing here? I thought she would be well on her way to Orson to wallow in her disappointment over Cole."

Whisper butted his shoulder with hers. "Be prepared to be blown away."

He chuckled as his aunt Beverly exited her vehicle and

walked toward them in her high heels, white slacks and flowered blouse. "Trace, Whisper, I'm so glad I caught you."

Damn, she actually wanted to talk to them. He'd been hoping she was here to see her mother. "Hello, Aunt Beverly."

She pulled off her sunglasses as she walked up the three steps to the porch. "You were holding out on us, Trace."

"I was?" As was common, he had no clue where his aunt was coming from.

"Yes, about Whisper." She turned toward Whisper, who at least hadn't started to frown yet.

"What about her?" He wrapped his arm around Whisper's waist to be sure his aunt understood exactly what she meant to him. Whisper seemed perfectly happy that he did so, leaning against him.

His aunt took one of Whisper's hands and he cringed. Not a good move.

"That your Whisper Adams is the daughter of Annabelle Adams, the heiress who died in a plane crash twenty-two years ago. I would have never connected the dots if Hailey hadn't finally remembered where she'd seen Whisper's face before." His aunt turned her gaze on him even as he felt Whisper become stiff in his arms.

"It wasn't that she'd actually seen Whisper, but Hailey is in flight school and she studied up on Arizona small plane crashes and saw a photograph of Anabelle Adams. Whisper, or rather Melisandre, looks just like her mother. Imagine my surprise to learn you were actually dating an heiress."

Chapter Nine

Trace looked at Whisper, expecting her to deny it, but she didn't. In fact, her face revealed that she was this heiress. He stepped away, not quite ready to accept the full impact of her betrayal. "Why are you living in a trailer if you have money?"

She looked at him. "I've been in hiding. I have two cousins who won't stop looking for me. They want the money, so I had to go off the grid."

"See." His aunt continued as she clapped her hands together. "I knew it. Oh, I must tell your grandmother. Excuse me."

His aunt walked between them and into the house as if she hadn't just destroyed dreams he hadn't even admitted he had.

He stared at Whisper, who seemed preoccupied. "Were you going to tell me?"

She shook her head.

"Why not?" The pain in his heart built as the reality sank in. She was rich and he had nothing.

"It didn't matter. Like I said, I've been hiding. I didn't want *anyone* to know."

In other words, she didn't want him to know. "Why? Because I'm broke?"

"No, the money is a curse. It hounds me, making my life

difficult, forcing me off the grid and away from civilization. It always had…until I came here."

He thought of the trailer. It was state of the art inside. It had to cost as much as his grandparents' house. He was so blind. "So all along you could have been paying Cole rent to be on the land where your trailer is."

She frowned. "That's his land?"

Trace snorted. "Yes, and he wanted you off because he was afraid you would gain squatter's rights. Little did we know you could afford to pay rent, eliminating the whole issue."

"I didn't know that was an issue. I didn't know it was anyone's land up there." Her puzzled expression fueled his anger.

"No, you didn't because I was protecting you." He took another step back. "Hah. Stupid me. I even had Lacey working on getting Cole to change his mind."

"Trace, I don't understand why you're so upset. The fact that people know who I am, especially your aunt, is a lot worse than the fact that I have money."

He stared at her, not even trying to comprehend her logic. "Was it because I might lose everything? Did you pity me? Is that why you hid that little fact about having tons of money?"

She stared at him as if he'd morphed into a horse. "Why would it matter if you're broke? I don't understand why this is an issue."

"Because I love you, dammit! Because I thought we might have a future together. What an idiot I was." The confused look in Whisper's eyes was the last straw. She just didn't get it. Maybe she didn't get human emotions at all, only animal ones.

He turned on his heel and bounded down the steps of the porch, striding to the barn to saddle Lightyear.

"Come on, buddy, I need to run off some steam and you

are just the one to do it." Kicking the horse into a gallop, he headed toward Cole and Lacey's unfinished house.

His heart was tearing in half. Not only had she hidden her money from him, but she didn't grasp that he loved her. It was as if she'd never considered such a thing.

It was his own fault. He'd told himself he wouldn't get involved with a down-on-her-luck woman again and he did, only to discover it was worse than he thought. She had more money than he'd know what to do with.

Compared to what his wife had done, Whisper was by far the crueler of the two. His wife took everything he owned and left him with nothing. Whisper ripped out the only thing he had left to give, his heart.

Whisper stared after Trace as he disappeared. He loved her? She searched her heart for a responding feeling, but she had no idea what it would feel like. She liked how she felt around him, except it hurt inside that Trace was upset, just like she hurt when an animal was in pain.

The ache persisted. She'd talk it over with Uncle Joey when they got home. He could help her figure this out, and they needed to go home now. She didn't like that Trace's aunt knew who she was. That woman would tell everyone, if she hadn't already.

Shit, Trace was supposed to take her and Joey home. Now what was she going to do? Her gaze fell on Logan, who was watching Black Jack in the corral. He would have to do.

In no time, she and Joey were on the road with Logan. She was surprised how quickly he'd agreed to help them and by how gentle he was with Joey. Maybe he wasn't all bad, even if he still had that anger boiling right beneath the surface.

Logan slowed down as the speed limit dropped, signaling

the town line. "We need to stop at Dr. Jenna's and let her or her staff know we don't need her help."

"Okay." She liked Jenna because she helped animals and always did what was best for them.

Logan pulled up outside the vet's office. "Would you mind running in and letting them know?"

She frowned. "Why don't you do it? I'm in the middle here."

Logan looked uncomfortable. "I'd rather you did."

"You don't like Dr. Jenna, do you?"

Logan's hands loosened on the steering wheel then gripped it again. "It's not that I do or don't like her. We just don't see eye-to-eye when it comes to horses. If I go in there and she's there, we'll just get into an argument. If you don't mind waiting for that to be over, I can do it."

Really? Why was she suddenly reminded of those teenagers she had nothing in common with?

She looked at Joey. He rolled his eyes before jerking his head, yes.

"Let me out."

Since she sat in the middle, Logan had to exit for her to leave the vehicle. She ran up to the porch of the vet's office and opened the door. She proceeded to the desk. "I have a message for Dr. Jenna. Tell her Last Chance doesn't need her to come out."

The older woman with gray hair smiled. "Actually, she just got back." The woman rose. "Let me get her for you."

"No, that's okay, just…" She gave up, the woman having walked away already.

She turned around to see who else was there. Two people waited and one dog. She met the big pit bull's eyes and smirked. He was pretty happy to be there. That made one of them.

She turned back toward the desk at the sound of a door closing. Dr. Jenna hurried toward her. Instead of stopping at the desk, she came around and grabbed her arm. "Come."

Whisper frowned but let herself be pulled into a nearby exam room. As soon as Jenna closed the door, Whisper pulled away. "What is it? I just came to—"

"Those men came back."

Whisper's heart froze then kicked back in double-time. "Keith and Timmy?"

Jenna nodded. "They were waiting for me in the parking lot when I got back from a ranch call. They said they saw on the internet that you were at a party on Last Chance Ranch. They wanted to know if I'd ever seen you there."

Fear coursed through her veins. They knew she lived on that land. "What did you say?"

"I told them I hadn't seen you at all and asked them why they were looking for you again. They told me you were mentally unstable and if I saw you to call the police because you were dangerous."

Damn them. Once she was in police custody, they'd have her, her word against theirs.

Jenna grabbed her arm. "I pulled up in your truck. Luckily, they didn't investigate it, so as soon as they left, I brought it home and put it in the garage."

"Shit. I'm going to have to move again. Joey and I really liked it here."

"Maybe you shouldn't. Maybe it's time you stood up to them."

Whisper's gut started to burn with hurt at the prospect of disappearing again even as she shook her head. She needed to leave as soon as it was dark, so no one would see her pull the trailer onto the highway outside of town. She had a lot to do before then, including emptying the shed and digging up the money. "I can't chance it. Can you bring my truck to the trailer at sundown? You can have the ATV."

"I can, but are you sure you don't want to fight them? I can stand up for you as a witness to your sanity."

The offer was tempting, but she couldn't involve Jenna in her troubles. Keith and Timmy were dangerous. "No. We have to go. Thank you for warning me. I just hope I can leave in time."

Jenna finally nodded and gave her a hug.

Thanks to Lacey, Whisper had become used to hugs and embraced Jenna. She hadn't even realized it, but she had two friends she'd have to leave. Just another reason not to make friends.

When they parted, Jenna had tears in her eyes. "I'll be there at sunset."

"Thank you." Whisper left the exam room and walked into the waiting area. She glanced at the happy pit bull. What would happen to Faust and Viola and Sebastian? She wouldn't be around to see Motley's baby either. She swallowed hard as she moved to the window.

She scanned the road to see if Keith and Timmy were in sight, but it had been two years since they'd last caught up with her and she had no idea what vehicle they could be driving. Another disadvantage to being off the grid, she couldn't search public records for the car. Then again, they could easily rent a car.

Taking a deep breath, she walked out onto the porch. Her plan, if they saw her and headed for her, was to run.

All the way to the truck, she watched her surroundings, her heart pounding, expecting a hand to clamp on her shoulder at any moment.

Logan stepped out of the truck and she scooted in. Once he started driving again, she checked behind them, but no one followed.

"What are you looking for?"

She turned back around. "I was checking to see if anyone followed us."

Logan's brows lowered. "Why? What did Jenna say? She knows not to come to the ranch, right?"

"Damn, I forgot to tell her."

"What? You were in there a long time. What were you talking about? Horses? We better go back."

Whisper grabbed his arm. "No!"

"Whisper, you better tell me what's going on."

She looked over at Joey and he looked up. He wanted to know, too. He could probably feel her agitation.

"You need to get us home so I can pack up the trailer and leave. My two cousins know I'm living on Last Chance land and they will go over every square foot of it until they find me. My only chance is to get out of town tonight."

Logan didn't slow down, but he did scowl. "Why do you have to run away from your cousins?"

As briefly as she could, she explained the situation starting with the attempted kidnapping and finishing with the last attempt to have her committed. "If I'm committed or dead, they can legally inherit the money."

Logan turned onto the dirt path to the trailer. "Holy shit, Whisper. Does Trace know?"

Trace. She wouldn't get to say goodbye to him. Her heart constricted, tightening in her chest just like it had when Joey told her that her parents had died. Oh, damn. She must love him. She didn't want to leave him and it hurt. She shook her head at Logan's question, her throat too tight to allow her to speak.

Joey grunted and she looked at him, unable to hide her tears. Joey moved his eyes from side to side telling her no, not to leave. But she couldn't allow them to hurt him. She had to think about more than just herself.

"You need to tell Trace. I don't think he'd want you to leave."

She swallowed hard. "I don't think he cares anymore. Remember when you told me you'd find me if I broke his heart. I already did that."

Logan parked in front of the trailer but made no move to get out. "Then you need to un-break it."

"I don't think that's possible, especially not now. Now let me and Joey out."

Logan didn't budge. "Listen, Cole has a friend in the police department."

"I know. I met detective Anderson. He interrogated me at the New Year's Eve party last night. I don't think he's on my side since I admitted to wanting to kill that animal abuser who hurt Lacey's horse."

The one hand Logan had on the steering wheel loosened and gripped it again. "You just said what we were all thinking. Let us at least talk to Sean."

That wasn't going to get her anywhere and she knew it, but Logan wasn't going to let her out and time was ticking. She had Sal in her jeans, but there was no way she could shoot Trace's brother. "I'm leaving as soon as it's completely dark. If you can work some kind of magic with the detective let me know before then, otherwise, tomorrow morning we'll be long gone.

She sensed Joey's relief next to her. She'd have to make sure he didn't get his hopes up.

Logan let go of the steering wheel, climbed out of the truck and held the door open for her.

A shot rang out and he went down. "Logan!"

Whisper leaned over to see Trace's brother lying still, facedown on the desert floor. "Shit, shit, shit." She stayed low, beneath the dash, and unbelted Joey. Laying him down on the seat, she lowered herself to the cab floor and met her uncle's worried gaze.

"I'm going to get you out of this safe and sound, old man. No need for concern."

Joey grunted.

"Yeah, we're *all* going to get through this." She glanced at the now vacant driver seat, worry making her stomach feel like she swallowed a bees' nest. She met Joey's gaze again. "You saw it. They made the first shot."

He jerked his head.

She needed to figure out where her cousins were shooting from and draw them away from Logan. She opened the passenger side door fast.

Another shot was fired near it. She crawled to the edge of the truck and studied the ground. There. There was a hole where the bullet hit the dirt. Thanks to the dry earth, it was easy to see the angle.

She closed her eyes, picturing where they had parked in relation to where the shot was fired from. Her cousins had to be standing in the bed of a pickup truck in the Joshua Tree forest because there was nothing high enough and nothing to hide behind in that direction. Keith may be smart at hacking accounts, but he knew very little about guns. It meant Timmy was shooting. Unfortunately, he was an excellent shot.

Making a guess as to where they might be, she stayed on the floor and put her gun's barrel in the crease in the door where it wouldn't be obvious. She dared not stick her head out to aim, but she angled her hand the best she could and fired.

"Fucking Christ, that bitch almost shot me." Keith's voice was loud and clear and not that far away.

Timmy yelled out, "Millie! Come out and leave your weapon in the truck and we won't hurt anyone else. All we need is you."

That wasn't going to happen. Instead she focused on where the voices came from and angled the gun again and shot.

"Shit!"

Silence followed her last shot. She itched to look above the dashboard. If she stayed below it, she was a sitting duck. One of them could keep firing while the other sneaked up to the truck. Plus, she only had a few more rounds. She looked above the seat to see a rifle hanging there. *Thank you, Logan.*

She crawled back to the other side to check on him. He lay in the same position, but blood seeped out from under his leg and a stain was growing on his calve. If his shin was shattered, he was in trouble.

She could sense the pain he was in, but the low-grade anger he carried around with him was much stronger, like a full-blown rage. It shook her and she crawled back to where Joey was. She had to take a chance to peek. Instead of looking over the dashboard, she shot again and immediately pulled the gun away and looked through the opening.

She couldn't see anything. Damn it. There was no return shot. She needed to draw their fire. Taking off her boot, she raised it in front of the passenger seat.

A shot shattered the front window of the truck, but the tempered glass kept it all intact in a spider web fashion, sparing Joey any glass shards. The bullet buried itself in the seat cushion two feet above his body and gave her the exact location of the shooter. Unfortunately, he was on foot and too close.

~~*~~

Trace let Lightyear run, the rhythm of the horse a soothing balm to his tattered heart. Maybe he'd expected too much from Whisper. After all, he was technically still married, plus her experience with men was limited. Hell, her experience with people was minimal compared to most Arizonans.

Still, he thought he at least had a special place in her life, especially after their night together. Shit, he could make up every excuse in the world, but the fact was, she fascinated him. And she held his heart.

The money was an issue. He was hurt because she didn't trust him to tell him, but his pride smarted to know he couldn't provide for her, not yet anyway, and she didn't even need him to. It was the complete opposite scenario from the wife who was leaving him.

Everything about Whisper was different. That's why he was so attracted to her. The idea that she might not love him in return hurt too much.

The echo of a shot caught his attention. He slowed Lightyear, trying to figure out where it came from. It could be hunters. Hell, his own grandfather was out hunting today, but he'd gone north. Not hearing anything else, he turned Lightyear around to head back. He'd told Whisper he'd bring her and Joey to her trailer and had left her at the ranch house. Someone else might have driven her back, but he should—

Another shot rang out and he held Lightyear back. Two more followed.

That wasn't hunting.

Whisper's words on the porch, which he didn't pay attention to then, chilled him now. *I've been in hiding. I have two cousins who won't stop looking for me. They want the money, so I had to go off the grid.*

Fuck. If Whisper was home, she was in danger. He turned Lightyear toward the canyon wall. And if she wasn't? That meant she was safe and he had to get his head on straight and figure out how to make her love him just as soon as he investigated what was going on in the middle of the desert. The echoes made it hard to know where the shots were coming from. For all he knew, they were in town and he was a fool.

But once Lightyear made it over the rim and another shot was fired, his gut tightened with fear. He had to slow the horse to get through the Joshua trees, and he flinched as three additional shots rang out. How many people? How many guns?

When he got close enough to see the trailer, he quietly pulled out his rifle and slipped off Lightyear. At the sight of Logan's truck and the window with a bullet hole through it, his muscles tensed. Two of the most important people in his life were in danger.

Another shot was fired from the truck's passenger door. That meant at least one person was alive. The question was, which one? If Logan brought Whisper home, then Joey was around too. Was he in the truck or already in the trailer? Fuck.

Frustrated at not being able to see anyone, he worked his way around the long way, toward what he hoped were the shooters. The Joshua trees offered little cover, but he had to do something. Even now someone could be dying. He couldn't even contemplate having someone already beyond his help.

As he passed two Joshua trees next to each other, he caught sight of one of the shooters walking toward the truck with no cover. Trace dropped to the ground. Luckily, the thin man with the long goatee was too focused on the truck and getting close to it.

From this angle, Trace could see someone lying on the ground. His heart stopped. It was the driver side. Logan? Even as his heart insisted on pumping the pain of loss through his veins, the person moved beneath the truck.

He released the breath he held. Logan and Whisper were both alive. A surge of adrenaline ricocheted through him. There were two shooters. If he could distract them, then Whisper or Logan, whoever was in the vehicle, could take down one while he took down the other. The problem was, from where he crouched he could only see the man with the goatee.

And that man was getting too close to the truck. Trace had to move now or the person inside was dead. He jumped up and ran through the trees quietly, watching the goatee man. As he stepped into the clearing, he yelled, "Stop right there!"

It all happened fast. The other shooter shouted and Trace turned, shooting a large bald man in the shoulder. At the same time a shot was fired behind Trace. He spun to see the man with the goatee fall to the ground, clutching his knee even as blood dripped from his forearm. Trace ran to the vehicle and stared.

Whisper was on the floor, Joey lay on his side on the seat and Logan looked up at him from beneath his truck. Relief threatened to buckle his knees, but once ascertaining they were all alive, he ignored the crying of the shooter with the goatee and grabbed up the man's gun.

Whisper jumped from the truck and threw herself at him. "Trace! I love you." She didn't give him time to respond. Her lips planted firmly on his.

He wrapped his arms around her and squeezed her hard as their tongues locked, his heart beating faster than a rattler's rattle.

"Ahem, do you think someone could give a wounded man a hand up?"

At Logan's voice, Whisper spun out of his arms. "You're alive!" She was so pleased Trace had to chuckle, knowing how the two didn't get along very well.

"Whisper, get the gun from that bald man while I help Logan."

"Right." She ran over to the man he'd shot in the shoulder while he bent and helped his brother to stand on one leg.

"That looks like it hurts. Let's get you to the tailgate." He helped Logan to the back of the pickup and opened the gate. "Now stay there."

Logan held up one hand. "Hell, you don't have to tell me twice."

Trace started for the bald man when a grunt from the cab reminded him there was someone else who was happy to be alive. He leaned in and brought Joey up to a sitting position. "Hey, Joey. Good to see you alive and well."

Joey rolled his eyes and Trace gave another chuckle of relief.

Whisper came back with the bald man's gun. She handed it to him with one hand while she pointed back with the other. "The one you shot is Timmy and the sneaky one here that Logan and I hit is Keith. They're my cousins. They've never gone this far before."

Trace glowered at the Keith. "And now they've sealed their fate. They shot my brother and the truck is excellent evidence they wanted to shoot you as well. They aren't going to bother you again where they're headed."

She smiled, that heart-stopping smile that he'd only seen once before. "I meant what I said. I love you. I didn't realize it until I thought I would have to disappear again. The thought of leaving you cut into my heart. I get it now."

For a passionate declaration of love, it lacked subtly, but from Whisper, it was music to his ears. He pulled her against him. "Hell, woman, I love you too."

"Good. Now kiss me."

He laughed before lowering his lips and giving her everything she demanded…and more.

Epilogue

He grasped Whisper's hand as they sat in the kitchen of the ranch house and laughed at Lacey, who had her hands covering her ears as she explained the noise level in the house the day before.

Cole made a big show of pulling Lacey's hands away from her head. "No need for that this afternoon…sweet pea."

Whisper squeezed his hand but didn't look at him.

Lacey growled. "I can't believe my father told you about my old nickname. I outgrew it ages ago."

"I like it." Whisper's voice was quieter than usual, a subtlety he was becoming more adept at catching.

"Why?" He was learning to ask about everything, otherwise his amazing woman wouldn't think to share.

She looked at him. "My dad used to call me that."

As much as he wanted to take her in his arms, he'd also learned she didn't like that when she felt vulnerable. Instead, he gave her a self-deprecating smirk. "I get that. My dad used to call me piglet because he said as a baby I ate more food then he could afford." He smiled sadly at the memory. "Luckily, he dropped it by time I was five, or I may have tried to prove him right." He winked.

Cole looked at his wife, the newlywed glow still obvious. "Then I guess I should just call her by my nickname for her."

"Cole Hatcher, don't you dare." Lacey lifted her hand to cover his mouth as if she had any chance of stopping him.

Trace couldn't resist. "You have to tell us now."

Getting up from her chair, Lacey doubled her efforts to stop her husband as he opened his mouth.

Finally, Cole laughed. "She's my Racy Lacey."

Lacey smacked him on the arm. "I can't believe you told them."

Cole pulled his wife onto his lap. "They won't tell, right, Trace?"

He chuckled. "No, your secret is safe with me."

Whisper's brow furrowed. "Why is she racy?"

Cole opened his mouth, but Lacey spoke before he could say a word. "I like to wear sexy lingerie under my clothes." She looked back at Cole. "He really likes it."

Trace could tell Whisper's mind was working a mile a minute just from her concentration. When she turned to him, he found himself anxious to find out what she would say.

"Would you like that?"

His cock started to harden just at the suggestion. "I would, but just once in a while. Surprise me."

Whisper nodded. "Good." She looked at Lacey. "You can help me pick some out."

Lacey laughed. "You bet. I'll show you my favorite stores. We can go next weekend."

His cock was now rock hard, but then he grinned at Lacey. He could just imagine Whisper asking Lacey about each and every product in that type of store. "That should be interesting."

Lacey waved him away. "Trust me, Trace, I'm not easily embarrassed."

He raised his brow even as the image of Whisper holding up an anal toy appeared in his head. Shit, now his jeans were stretched to their limit. He needed a change in topic. "So you were saying how thrilled you were that it was quiet today. Is everyone gone?"

Cole nodded. "No idea how that happened. We didn't even arrange it. Besides our chores, the only thing we had planned was you two coming over for lunch."

"And it was a great lunch, Lacey. Thank you." Trace looked at Whisper. "We wanted to talk to you about paying rent for the property we have the two trailers on. Now that the divorce is final, my ranch should sell soon and I'll receive half the profit, so I'm happy to make monthly payments. I know that's important to you." He kept his eyes on Cole.

Cole snorted. "First, you're family, so I'm not worried. Second, you two have done enough as it is. And third, I asked detective Anderson about the squatter laws and it's far more complicated than I realized. You two are fine up there. Besides, you gave old Billy a new purpose in life."

"What? How?" Trace looked from Cole to Lacey.

Lacey grinned. "He was fine being Grandpa's helper whether it was carting his hunting gear around or being his caddy on the golf course, but I guess those two pursuits don't allow for much talking."

Trace laughed. "Oh yes, that old man loves to talk. Hell, he even does it in his sleep." He looked at Whisper. "Remember how I told you I'd slept on the couch before?"

She nodded.

"That was because I roomed with old Billy and between him talking in his sleep and his snoring, I was getting less shut-eye than Logan. I figured two grumps in the house was one too many, so I would sneak down and stretch out on the couch."

He turned his attention back to Cole. "So why does Billy feel visiting Uncle Joey is his new calling?"

Whisper smirked. "Because Billy can talk all day and Joey doesn't interrupt. Joey is loving it. Billy is even reading the paper to him. I should have thought of that."

Lacey jumped in before Trace could say anything. "You had a few too many other things to think about. Speaking of, now that your cousins are in jail, I'm thinking we need to do something for Sean. The poor guy lost both Christmas and New Year's days to trouble on Last Chance ranch."

Cole grinned. "At least this time it was Trace's trouble and not ours. We've used up all our credits with that man."

Whisper's eyes lit. "We should give him a week at Poker Flat Nudist Resort."

Cole coughed and Trace chuckled, even as Lacey shook her head. "I'm pretty sure Sean's wife wouldn't go for that. Besides, as a detective, he can't accept anything too expensive."

Whisper's shoulders slumped. "There goes my other idea."

Ever since Whisper was free to put her money in a bank and other financial institutions, she was more than ready to spend it. The new trailer she bought for them with three slide outs instead of two, and the trust she set up for Last Chance horses with the help of Lacey was proof of that. He squeezed her hand to get her attention. "Maybe it needs to be something that can't be bought."

"Like what?" Her gaze filled with curiosity.

"How about public recognition. We could each write a letter to the Police Chief recognizing Sean for his good deeds."

Cole pointed at him. "I like that."

"Me, too." Lacey smiled and looked to Whisper who gave a nod.

"Then it's settled. We'll do that." Trace was very grateful for Sean's help. The detective even said they could spare Joey having to be a witness, but Whisper wanted her uncle to testify, to bring home exactly what kind of people her cousins were.

Whisper stood up. "We'll leave now."

He looked at her then at Cole and Lacey before he shrugged and stood also. "I guess we have to go."

Whisper nodded. "Yes. They want to have sex and there is no one else around, so we should leave."

Lacey turned two shades of red and Cole hid his embarrassment by setting Lacey on her feet and standing as well.

Trace grinned. "Hmm, that's not a bad idea." He pulled Whisper against his side.

She looked at him, her eyes darkening with the idea. "That was my thought."

Cole laughed as he walked around the table to shake hands. "I'm glad you two are our neighbors."

Trace shook then grabbed up his hat and headed for the door. "Better that than living with you, cousin." Opening the door for Whisper, he stepped aside and she walked through. "I hope for your sakes the house is finished soon." He jogged to catch up with Whisper.

Cole and Lacey stood on the porch as he raced down the steps to open the truck door for his woman. She just shook her head at him and climbed in.

He closed her door and tipped his hat at the newlyweds. Walking around the truck to his door, he smirked at the carport standing next to the barn. Black Jack stood in its shade, taking a light nap. How had they all managed to function before Whisper?

Jumping into his truck, he waved one more time and drove toward home. The trip was a quiet one. Another change in his life he'd adjusted to.

As he turned onto the dirt road that would bring them back to Whisper's old trailer and the new one parked within sight of it, she spoke for the first time since getting into the truck. "Why did they say Keith and Timmy were *your* trouble? They were after me, not you."

He smiled. "Because you are my responsibility now, so it all fell squarely on my shoulders."

"That's not true. My cousins were *my* problem."

He slowed, bringing the truck to a stop halfway down the three-mile dirt road. "That may be true, but it's my job to take care of *you*."

She glowered at him and opened her mouth, but he pressed his finger against her lips.

"And it's *your* job to take care of me."

Her face changed and he knew he'd guessed right. He loved trying to stay one step ahead of her.

When she licked his finger, he started. Now that he hadn't expected.

She grabbed his wrist and sucked his finger into her mouth.

His cock immediately started to swell. "If you keep that up, I'm going to strip you right here."

She paused and that special gleam came into her eyes. "Great idea."

Before he could respond, she'd whipped her shirt over her head and her breasts caught and held his attention. He quickly unzipped his pants. Whisper was never one to slowly take off clothes. She said she liked touching skin to skin. Hell, so did he.

When she was naked, she opened the door and stepped out of the truck.

Shit, what was she doing now?

He laid his hat on the dashboard and pulled his t-shirt off over his head. When his face cleared the neckline, Whisper slammed her seat back. In her arms was the emergency blanket he kept in the truck. She stepped away and closed the door.

Toeing off his boots, he pulled down his jeans and jumped out stark naked to find her. He didn't have far to look.

In the bed of the truck was Whisper, completely naked and sitting on the blanket. She looked like a wild woman, her black hair loose and messy about her bare shoulders and a predatory look on her face.

He sat on the tailgate and swiveled around to face her.

"I want to make love out here where it's free." She opened her arms wide, as if she could feel nature itself.

"I'm happy to make love to you anywhere you want." He crawled toward her, letting her determine what they would do. He loved it when she wanted to experiment. He definitely needed to make reservations at Poker Flat for his wild woman.

He'd thought about introducing her to sex toys on Valentine's Day, but with Lacey taking her out next week, she could choose what she wanted to try first. One thing he didn't have to worry about with Whisper, was wondering what she thought of something.

When he knelt in front of her, she surprised him by turning her back, pulling her hair forward over one shoulder and kneeling. "Touch me."

He grinned. Placing his hands on her shoulders, he ran them down her back, smoothing them over her skin and rounding over her ass to her thighs. He purposefully didn't go near her favorite spots to build her anticipation.

Again he ran his hands over her back, but this time brushed her sides as well, barely touching the edges of her breasts. When he got to her ass, he squeezed each cheek, separating them from each other a bit before running his hands to the insides of her thighs and down, still avoiding what she wanted most.

"You're teasing me, aren't you?" Her voice was even more husky with her libido revved up.

"Yup." This time he knelt a little closer and brought his hands down her arms, under them, along her sides, and around the fronts of her thighs, careful not to touch her with his body.

"Trace. I'm wet for you."

His cock moved at her statement. "Really?" He moved his body up against hers, his erection nestled on her ass, his chest against her back. "Do you want me to feel you?"

She nodded, her breath coming out short now. He started at her shoulders and smoothed his hands over her breasts, under them and down her waist before grabbing her thighs and pulling her hips tight against him.

"Oh."

Finally, he moved both hands toward her pussy. She was more than wet. With his left hand, he slipped a finger inside her opening. With his right, he spread her moisture over her clit and proceeded to rub it gently.

As her head fell back on his shoulder, he wondered at the circumstances that had brought them together like this. Body to body, beneath the warm Arizona sun in the back of his pickup where he would take her, body and soul to nirvana and back. They'd come a long way from her holding him at gun point to him holding her in his arms.

Her head came off his shoulder. "I want you inside now."

So did he. Slipping his fingers from her, he turned her slightly so she faced the side of the truck. "Hold on."

She bent forward and braced herself.

Spreading her legs father apart, he pressed his cock against her opening. "Ready?"

She took a deep breath. "Yes."

He grasped her hips, knowing full well she couldn't wait. He kneaded her skin. Upping her need like a race car driver revving an engine.

"Trace, please."

He rubbed his thumbs back and forth across her hips, making her wait. He could barely hold on himself, so he pressed forward just a bit, just enough to push her opening wider, but he held on, daring himself not to plunge.

Whisper moaned in frustration and wiggled her hips, trying to push back.

"Shh, wait for it. Let it build."

She moaned again, but he kept her hips where he wanted them as her wetness seeped out and over his cock. He gritted his teeth, focusing on the feel of her entrance. She loved it when he surprised her. If he could just hold on another few seconds.

He couldn't. He pulled his hips back then slammed forward. "Yesss!"

His orgasm rose up. *No, not yet.* He moved his hands from her hips to her breasts and squeezed them lightly before finding her hard nipples and pinching them. Her hips pulled forward and banged back against him, pushing his finale too close to the edge.

He couldn't stop. She pulled back and thrust her hips toward him. He let go of her breasts and grasped the side of the truck on either side of her. Rhythmically, he pumped hard, the feel of her body against his chest spurring him on, making it difficult to hold back.

But when her sheath tightened around him, he let loose his own pleasure and pounded into the woman he loved, his world complete…perfect.

Whisper's screams of ecstasy were lost in the vastness of the upper desert, and he held her to her orgasm as long as he could. When her body quieted, he knelt back, taking her with him, keeping them connected as she sat on his lap.

She flipped her hair back, most of it landing on his back

and the soft feel of it sent a trill of excitement to his cock, making it jump inside her.

She reached down between her legs and touched him. "You're still hard."

"No, I'm getting hard again."

"Hmmm." She wriggled against him. "I like that."

He chuckled. "You are insatiable, but I know exactly what to do."

"What?" He could hear the excitement in her voice.

"This." He reached one hand down and flicked at her clit. "Are you ready to come for me again?"

"Always."

He grinned against her hair before he leaned his head to the side of her neck and kissed her at the same time his fingers twirled around her hard nub and her breathing escalated.

"Always" sounded good to him.

The End

Read on for an excerpt from Cowboy's Match

Chapter One

Cole Hatcher ignored the yellow and orange streaks of the Arizona sunset and focused on the same colors rising from the burning building as flames moved with the breeze. He spoke into the radio. "Move the two and a half inch to the northwest corner."

Two firefighters lugged the hose toward the base of the fire at the edge of the partially constructed building. Not more than fifteen feet away was a pile of old barn wood just waiting to ignite.

Stepping back toward the engine, Cole received a nod from Mason, the fire engine monitor, before speaking into the radio again. "Tanker, is the dry hydrant hooked yet?"

"Almost." The reply was not the answer Cole wanted. They would need more water than an engine and tanker could provide, and the chance of the winds picking up once the sun disappeared were better than a horse getting loose through an open gate.

As if on cue, the whinny of several frightened horses in the nearby barn caused him to tense. There was no way he would let the fire spread that way.

The radio clicked before a firefighter's voice came through. "We're hooked."

Cole breathed easier. As long as he had water, he could put this baby out. "Good. Stay with the tanker. I'll need someone to come over here and grab the one and a half inch with Clark." He watched as Clark unwound the hose, already heading toward the construction site that hid behind the smoke and flames of the fire's onslaught.

Glancing back to where the tanker was parked thirty yards away, Cole swore. "What the hell?" Coming up the hill along the dirt road his trucks had just rolled in on, were at least a half dozen golf carts filled with naked people.

He stifled a laugh. What'd they think this was? A campfire? A Wild West show? Did they plan to make s'mores? This would be a story to tell at the firehouse for sure. Still, as with all spectators to a disaster, it wasn't safe for them to be there. He silently wished he had a radio to communicate with the owner, who had enough sense to keep the resort guests from getting any closer.

For over a year, he'd been curious about the Poker Flat Nudist Resort, but Clark had been chosen to give the fire extinguisher class to all the employees before the resort opened three months ago, and Cole had no official reason to come check it out. Fighting a fire wasn't a good way to learn about a place. Whatever this new construction was, it was toast. His concern was with the barn and the horses and which way the wind would blow next.

An explosion from the fire shook the ground as flames shot into the air. "Shit." What the hell did they have in that unfinished building? The two men with the smaller hose lost their footing and fell, but since they hadn't made it to the fire yet, they were unharmed.

He'd be damned if he'd put his men in harm's way when no lives were at stake.

He turned toward the owner and motioned her closer, then faced the burning construction site. As the sky behind the fire turned a dull pink, the breeze picked up, changing the direction of the flames toward the open desert. Good for the horses, but not for wildfire potential. It'd been the driest summer on record. October temperature highs had finally dropped below triple digits and the nights were already getting cold, but there had been no rain during monsoon season.

Cole spoke into the radio again. "I need the two and half inch to lay down a curtain between the building and the open desert on your side."

"Got it." The two firefighters adjusted their hose and started a continual spray, wetting and cooling the area toward the open desert even as the men with the one and a half inch hose moved in to cover the fire base.

"Lieutenant, you wanted us?" The female voice had him turning around.

He'd forgotten he'd called over the owner. At least she and the cowboy with her were dressed. "You need to get those people out of here. I can't control the fire's embers and right now the wind is picking up."

The tall man nodded. "I'll take care of that." He immediately strode toward the golf cart brigade.

Cole turned his attention to the woman. "I've got my men focused on keeping the fire from spreading to your barn or out into the desert. A wildfire would be catastrophic, but we won't be able to save the building."

She waved her hand as if it meant little to her. "I'm not worried about the building as long as everyone is safe."

"Have you accounted for all your employees and guests?"

"Yes."

Another explosion had Cole turning away to check on his men. A voice came across his radio. "What the fuck is in here? A chemical lab?"

Cole frowned. He'd never thought of how convenient it would be to have a meth lab out at a nudist resort. He'd make sure the police investigated the place in case there had been illegal activity.

He looked at the owner. "How many more explosions should we expect?"

She frowned. "We had one before you arrived, that's what alerted me to the fire, but there shouldn't be anything that would explode over there. The plywood for the roof was completed, but they hadn't even set the windows in yet. All that was there was whatever the construction crew left."

"Do you have electricity out there yet?"

She shook her head.

Shit. "Gasoline for their generator." He spoke into his radio again. "Possible gas containers."

A gust of wind compounded his problems and he quickly repositioned his men. A siren could barely be heard in the distance, but the red and blue lights of a sheriff department car reflected far into the desert. About time they got here.

Cole spared a glance to where the golf carts had been parked and was relieved to see only a few left, but he scowled as a young woman with golden hair moved toward him and the owner, a tray of food and drinks in her hands. Shit, didn't these people realize this was a working fire? This was dangerous!

A third explosion rocked the ground and he spun in time to see a gust of wind pick up the roiling flames and throw them toward his men. He pressed the button on his radio. "Fall back!"

One man stumbled backward, catching his foot on the old barn wood and lost his grip on the hose. The other firefighter struggled with it before he went down too.

"Fuck." Cole sprinted to his men, pulling them back by their coats as the flames licked at their boots. The barn wood caught, feeding the fire.

Once his men were out of harm's way, he tackled the flailing line. A loose hose was a danger in its own right.

"Lieutenant, do you want us on the wood pile?" The question came through his radio.

Cole slammed his body onto the hose before replying, "Negative. Keep that curtain up."

The two firefighters that had been blown down regained their feet and grabbed the hose. "Thanks, Lieutenant."

He released his hold. "Pull back and soak that pile. If the wind shifts again, I don't want the barn catching."

The men nodded.

Cole turned around and strode back to the engine. The two women were still there. This wasn't a movie. Didn't they have any common sense?

After checking with Mason to be sure the water pressure was steady, he approached his audience, irritation growing at the petite stature of the blonde. Someone so delicate didn't belong at a working fire, but like the owner, at least she had clothes on. "Ladies, you need to get back." He pointed to the rise the golf carts had congregated on earlier.

The blonde smiled. "Selma sent over churros and iced tea for your men in case they need something."

Cole's blood froze. *That voice.* He studied the woman and his heart stumbled inside his chest. Her shapely figure proved she'd grown into a delectably curvy woman as he'd always expected she would, but her face was almost the same, just more refined. "Lacey Winters?"

Her brows furrowed and her button nose wrinkled as she peered back at him. Had he really changed so much in eight years? Yeah, probably. He'd been a bean pole last he'd seen her…the night he broke it off with her.

She gave up trying to figure out who he was. "I'm sorry. Do I know you?"

He should let it go. No need to dredge up the past. He had a fire to control.

His pulse went into overdrive. Another fire. It couldn't be coincidence. He scowled at her. "You should. I'm Cole, Cole Hatcher."

Even in the reflection of the flames, her face turned pasty white and he kicked himself for revealing his identity. All he needed now was a fainting woman to contend with.

"You two know each other?" The other woman leaned on one hip, her concern for Lacey evident in the look she gave him.

At the owner's voice, Lacey recovered her color. Actually, her face changed from white to an angry flush in a matter of seconds. It reminded him of a flashover.

"Not that I want to know him." Lacey handed the tray over to the owner and stepped up to him. She poked her index finger into his chest. Hard. "So, Cole Hatcher. Are you going to accuse me of setting this fire? After all, I'm here, on the same property. It's not like you need evidence or anything. Feel free to assume the worst. I'm sure it helps to justify the way you treated me." She pulled back as if touching him made her feel sick. "Good luck with that." Turning on her heel, she stalked off, her hips swaying enticingly until he remembered where he was and who he was looking at.

"So *you're* the one who broke her heart." The owner studied him briefly then set the tray on the ground and followed after Lacey.

Shit.

Cowboy's Match

http://www.lexipostbooks.com/cowboys-match/

For updates, sneak peeks, and special prizes, sign up to receive the latest news from Lexi at http://eepurl.com/D3MqT

Also by Lexi Post

Contemporary Cowboy Romance

Cowboys Never Fold
(Poker Flat Series: Book 1)
Cowboy's Match
(Poker Flat Series: Book 2)
Cowboy's Best Shot
(Poker Flat Series: Book 3)
Cowboy's Break
(Poker Flat Series: Book 4)
Wedding at Poker Flat
(Poker Flat Series: Book 5)

Christmas with Angel
(Poker Flat Series Book 2.5, Last Chance Series: Book 1)
Trace's Trouble
(Last Chance Series: Book 2)
Fletcher's Flame
(Last Chance Series: Book 3)
Logan's Luck
(Last Chance Series: Book 4)
Dillon's Dare
(Last Chance Series: Book 5)

Riley's Rescue
(Last Chance Series: Book 6) *Coming Soon*
Aloha Cowboy
(Island Cowboy Series: Book 1)

Military Romance

When Love Chimes (Broken Valor Series: Book 1)
Poisoned Honor (Broken Valor Series: Book 2)

Paranormal Romance

Masque
Passion's Poison
Passion of Sleepy Hollow
Heart of Frankenstein

Pleasures of Christmas Past
(A Christmas Carol Series: Book 1)
Desires of Christmas Present
(A Christmas Carol Series: Book 2)
Temptations of Christmas Future
(A Christmas Carol: Book 3)
One of A Kind Christmas
(A Christmas Carol Series: Book 4)
On Highland Time (Time Weavers, Inc.: Book 1)

Sci-fi Romance

Cruise into Eden (The Eden Series: Book 1)
Unexpected Eden (The Eden Series: Book 2)
Eden Discovered (The Eden Series: Book 3)
Eden Revealed (The Eden Series: Book 4)
Avenging Eden (The Eden Series: Book 5)
Beast of Eden (Eden Series: Book 6) *Coming Soon*

About Lexi Post

Lexi Post is a New York Times and USA Today best-selling author of romance inspired by the classics. She spent years in higher education taking and teaching courses about the classical literature she loved. From Edgar Allan Poe's short story "The Masque of the Red Death" to Tolstoy's *War and Peace*, she's read, studied, and taught wonderful classics.

But Lexi's first love is romance novels. In an effort to marry her two first loves, she started writing romance inspired by the classics and found she loved it. From hot paranormals to sizzling cowboys to hunks from out of this world, Lexi provides a sensuous experience with a "whole lotta story."

Lexi is living her own happily ever after with her husband and her cat in Florida. She makes her own ice cream every weekend, loves bright colors, and you will never see her without a hat.

www.lexipostbooks.com